ENCHANTING THE DRYAD PRINCE

Kingdoms of Lore

ALISHA KLAPHEKE

CHAPTER 1
ISA

Isa wondered if this would be the day that she finally strangled someone with her bare hands. She hoped so. And it was important to stay positive.

Thin clouds churned above the ship like wraiths, and she adjusted her stance to keep from listing to the left as she hid a seashell behind a barrel of hard tack biscuits.

Eighteen months ago, after a storm destroyed her tapestry shop, she'd been desperate for food. The Brunes—masters of this ship—had told her they were headed to sea in search of treasure and investments, and that if she agreed to a period of indenture with them, she'd see the world. Her mind had whirled as she'd envisioned dragons, rubies the size of her face, and mysterious folk like dryad elves. She hadn't waited one single day before signing on the dotted line.

She rolled her eyes and pushed her black hair out of her eyes. At twenty-one, she should have been well on her way to success. Instead, she was a slave in all but the paperwork —paperwork that had undoubtedly been thrown into the waves by Seigneur Brune himself.

Thankfully, she had little Nico to love in the middle of this hell. He was a scrappy kid who was as trapped as she was, forced into indenture by a lack of options.

"I hid three treasures in our berth and on deck here," she said to the one individual not on her to-strangle list.

Nico had shut his eyes, as she'd requested, but now he opened those big blue beauties as she explained the game. She'd surreptitiously snatched a rose-striped seashell, a piece of sea glass, and an odd bit of bronze from the crew's fishing nets over the past two weeks. Nico loved small things like that, and it was about all she could do to help him smile once in a while. Poor fellow. He was an indentured servant like her.

"Once we each finish a duty," she continued, "we get two minutes to search while pretending to work. First of us to have two treasures gets to keep them all. Deal?" With her continually bleeding, chapped fingers, she tied her skirts up at the knee so she wouldn't trip going belowdecks or up the stairs to the forecastle.

Nico grinned, his freckles light on his tanned skin and his blue eyes shining like gems. "Deal. But I'll save one for you if I win." His gaze went all serious and it was enough to break her heart.

Isa kissed his mop of tangled hair. "You are so much nicer than I am."

"That's because you're a wild monster, remember?" Nico

laughed as he grabbed a bucket he'd used for emptying the galley slops from last night's meal. He hurried away as quickly as an underfed, beaten boy of nine years old could manage. When they'd first started talking, she'd told him she was a wild creature from the craggy cliffs of Wylfenden, who would shed her skin once a moon and become a boy-eating monster. She'd hoped to scare the lad into leaving her alone to wallow in her utter misery. But the boy's sweet smile and determined spirit in the face of their situation had grown on her, and now she had to admit that she loved him like a brother.

Her heart ached as she watched him disappear belowdecks. He'd perked up since she took him under her wing, but she feared what would happen if he grew sick again. His slight frame could only handle so much.

Isa took up her own bucket—this one filled with what she needed to start up Seigneur and Dame's iron heating grate—then she headed for their quarters. Seigneur Brune was captain as well as master of the ship, a man born to wealth but still ridiculously desperate for more gold, more rare finds, more, more, more. His wife, Dame Brune, was a vulture in a pretty dress. Her favorite pastime was picking the bones of her dead-in-spirit servants.

Slipping into the Brunes' quarters, Isa used the soft-footed steps she'd learned on the streets of Nid de Lapin.

Seigneur's rumbling snore stayed consistent as she woke the banked fire in the belly of their iron grate stove. She scuttled over to Dame's side of the bed to place a cleaned chamber pot in the space between the ropes holding up the down-stuffed mattress and the salt-stained floorboards.

She stood to leave, but a sharp voice stopped her.

"I told you to bring us bread to break our fast, little mouse. I bet you ate it when the kitchen master gave it to you."

Isa knew better than to argue. Her tongue touched the still-healing lump on her bottom lip, a wound Dame had given her three days ago for talking back. She nodded, anger rising in her blood like sparks.

"I forgot the bread. I'll get it now, Dame." Isa hurried out of the room and toward the galley. The morning sky was blood red and wispy; gray clouds flew above the ship. It was going to storm.

Voices rose as Isa clambered down the slick steps to belowdecks.

"You clumsy wretch." Ursane—part gray-haired head maid, part black stain on humanity as a whole—was no doubt yelling at Nico.

Anger kindled what felt like a dancing, crackling fire in Isa's middle and she swallowed. The sensation began as unpleasant but grew to be a powerful, positive feeling. The odd fire—as she'd always called it in her head—arose when she experienced other strong emotions too. She'd always been too afraid to ask anyone else to see if she was alone on that one or not. Trying to suppress her emotions, she fisted her hands as the corridor led to the galley.

Nico sat on the floor as he looked up at Ursane, his jaw set like it did when he was trying not to cry. Ursane's slim cheeks rose into a smile as she set her beating stick on her shoulder.

Strangling seemed like the best recourse, really.

"What did he do this time?" Isa said, unable to school her tone. "Look at you wrong? Sneeze? How dare he be a human?"

Ursane slapped her hard across the mouth, reopening the cut. Warm blood ran down Isa's chin, and she just let it flow as she glared. She didn't speak. Ursane's glittering eyes dared her to say a word so she could hit her again, or worse, go to Dame or Seigneur. It wouldn't just be split lips and scowls then.

Isa pushed a retort back down, then helped Nico to his feet. Source save him, he weighed less than ever.

Dame appeared at the door to the galley. "What is happening here?"

Ursane curtseyed. "Nothing you need to worry about, Dame."

Setting Nico down, Isa mimicked the move as quickly as she was able, and wiped the blood from her face with the back of her sleeve. Nico bowed his head. With a quick squeeze of Nico's shoulder, she urged him toward the breadbox and they began slicing up the last of the flatbread they'd brought from their stop in Khem.

Ursane and Dame left, their loathsome voices murmuring complaints about Isa and Nico as they walked down the corridor. "I have serious doubts about those two..."

"I..." Nico sniffed and rubbed his nose with the back of

his hand before slicing another piece of bread. "I didn't get to look for any of the treasures yet."

"They're not going to grow legs and walk away."

He giggled. "You sure?"

"Well, unless that one shell I picked up has a very shy inhabitant."

"Inhabitant?" He blinked up at her with those sky blue eyes.

"Someone who lives in a place."

She'd been doing her best to educate the boy. Her parents, who'd adopted her from a band of traveling merchants, had taught her well. Nico was smart, even if he'd spent the first part of his life in a rundown orphanage.

"We're almost through being their servants, Nico. You know that, right? Have you been keeping track?" She'd taught him to tally so he'd have their last day of indenture to look forward to in a more concrete way.

"Yes!" He held up the knife.

She raised an eyebrow and carefully lowered the blade back to the flatbread. "Soon, we'll be off on our own adventure."

It was all she wanted. Freedom for him and for her. Even if it came with more terrible struggles. Anything was better than this prison of a ship.

CHAPTER 2
VIRIDI

Under a copse of opal-leafed jeweltrees, Viridi ran his thorned fingertips through his tangled, black hair. The first stars of the night flickered through the sunset sky. Like all dryad elves' souls, his soul sang for the starlight, the glory of the distant realms tingling across his skin and waking him, clearing his mind. Smooth and comforting earth magic curled from the ground, up through his bare feet and legs.

It was as though the earth knew Viridi needed support when dealing with his father, the king.

"Just shift," Father said, looking up into Viridi's face. "You can do this." Using hands that boasted no thorns or wooden tips like Viridi's, he adjusted the branch crown braided into his golden hair. His scowl pulled at his fine features, making him look more wolf than dryad elf. "I want to see you in your full form so we can discover how powerful you truly are." He grinned in that wickedly pleased manner that Mother had always hated. Viridi remembered her shuddering at that grin when he was very young and still ignorant of Father's blazing need to control and submit anyone in his presence.

Viridi's chest tightened and he swallowed, flexing his sharp fingers. He didn't want this fate of his—to be the Thorned One, the monstrous protector of their people, the dryad elves. But he had been born to it and there was no shirking the duty when one's father was King Elagabalus, cutthroat ruler of all the dryad elves. Father planned to use Viridi as he saw fit and there was no mercy in the king's heart, not a shred of it.

"Father. You aren't listening. The jeweltrees...there is something wrong with them. The words they whisper into my mind aren't protective but violent."

"Violence is a necessary part of protecting one's people. You know that. Don't go soft on me, Son. We need to find you a mate. Even if it isn't your fated match. A strong dryad elf mate might thrust you into your full power. It's time to fully grow up. You are twenty years of age, long past pretending life is some pleasant party."

Viridi glared and fought the temper rising inside him, wrestling the deep magic that swirled in his blood. His fingers began to lengthen and a shiver rode down his spine. The only time he'd come close to fully shifting, he'd been lost to himself, his mind a blur of hunger and anger.

End him, the jeweltrees hissed into Viridi's mind. *He does not respect the power. End them all.*

"They are instructing me to end you," Viridi said,

hoping Father would finally understand that though the jeweltrees were supposed to be sentient, wise protectors of this island, set to help the Thorned One keep the dryad elves safe and healthy, the jeweltrees had instead grown twisted.

"Bah." Father waved a hand. "Once you fully shift and grow used to the feel of it, I'm sure your mind will meld with theirs and all will be well. The cliff tribes will no longer attempt to overthrow me then. The Thorned One that reigned with King Cali in the second age was known to be incredibly powerful, able to move entire forests with a word, to alter the very tides around the island." His wolflike eyes glittered.

Anger raked coals across Viridi's mind. "If you'd stop enslaving the cliff tribes' people just to extract more gold you don't need, they would cease their aggressions." The cliff tribes had attacked their village at daybreak twice in the last six moons.

"You think you know more of ruling than me, Son?" Father stepped closer, his breath hot on Viridi's face.

The danger in those eyes told Viridi to watch his words. Father wouldn't kill him; he was too useful. But there were ways to control a person—he'd do something to Viridi's friends or some such awful thing. Dew and Felix were going to meet Viridi here soon. He hoped they wouldn't arrive until after Father left.

In order to protect them, Viridi swallowed his retort and pushed back at the magic flowing from his heart. Not yet. If he could help it, he wouldn't shift fully until he knew more about why the jeweltrees felt so...wrong.

"Of course not, Father," he gritted out. "I would never question you. But I do wish you would consider leaving. The Pearl Isles would be perfect for our people. Then if I am wrong about the danger I pose in my fully shifted form, I will join you or send word for you to return. Please, consider it."

"I will not. And I won't hear you bring it up again. I will never leave my island. I own this land and everyone in it. No one is leaving. That conversation is closed."

Viridi pressed his eyes shut, wishing Father would consider it. Maybe if Felix found something in the scrolls to point to Viridi's concerns...

"Viridi. Shift. I command you as your king." He struck him with his staff and pain lanced across Viridi's arm as he opened his eyes to see Father's glare. "Show me your loyalty by shifting now. Now, Viridi."

You're the monster, he longed to say. But he wouldn't because that might mean the end of his friends' lives. "I'm trying, but I cannot," he lied.

Father stared for a moment, then his shoulders relaxed as if he'd given up. "Fine. But you must do so and soon." He turned to leave, but stopped and raised a finger. "I have a surprise for you tonight. Make certain you aren't late to the festivities."

Viridi bowed his head slightly, and at last, Father walked away.

For several minutes, Viridi worked to calm the Thorned

One power until finally he felt like himself once more. He breathed deeply, and an unusual twinge of excitement fluttered across his heart.

Dropping his hands to his sides, he stared over the starlit ocean. Even with his excellent eyesight, he saw nothing but the black expanse. No lightning-fed cloud banks. No large swells.

There had been ships in the past, pirates and adventurers who had heard of their rare and valuable jeweltrees with their pearly leaves. His people had successfully warded the island from sight and killed any who'd managed to find a way through the magical barrier. The jeweltrees were sacred; they couldn't be risked for any reason.

But Viridi didn't spot any sails or dark crafts on the starlit horizon.

So what was this strange anticipation inside him?

He touched the jeweltree beside him and the tree's leaves shivered in delight as his magic and the tree's melded and spun back into them both equally. The tree was honored to have housed him during that day—he could feel the truth of it. Where was the evil whispering now? He shook his head. It didn't make any sense. One minute, the jeweltrees were fine and the next, they wanted Viridi to destroy everyone.

A snap in the forest behind him had Viridi turning around. Felix walked into view and waved.

"What do you see out there?" Felix's pale eyes were bright in the deepening dark.

The familiar feeling of wishing he fit in washed through Viridi. Since birth, his pointed ears had been tipped in wood instead of flesh like all the other dryad elves' ears. From the first day, everyone had known Viridi was different.

But he could live with being different as long as he managed to truly protect his people. He only had to figure out what was happening with the jeweltrees.

Viridi and Felix turned from the softly cresting waves of the broad ocean and took up the fern-bordered trail toward their village, one of many on the island.

"Father encouraged me to fully shift into my Thorned One form."

"Tonight?" Felix looked around as if Father might spring from the stars' shadows. The scar that ran across the left side of his mouth reflected the scant moonlight.

"Yes. You just missed him. Thank the gods."

A thin sliver of moon shyly cast its own glow as the night progressed. The oaks and pines shuffled in greeting as they passed. Felix asked for details about Viridi's conversation with Father and he told him everything. Since they were younglings, they'd been close, keeping nothing from one another. They walked the winding trail toward the village, keeping to the route that skirted everyone's home trees and the more commonly traveled paths.

"I read over the scrolls about other shifter beings," Felix said. "They were mostly focused on dragon shifters."

"Of course."

"I have only been able to find mentions of the two

Thorned Ones with no detail beyond what you already know."

That the Thorned Ones of the past could shift and unshift at will. "Maybe I will gain better control as I age."

His mind whirled with possibilities on how to solve the puzzle of the jeweltrees. He wished Mother hadn't died from the skirmish with the cliff tribes. She would have had ideas on how to help him learn about his fate and how to conquer its challenges. Viridi had thought Father would aim for peace after Mother's death, but that thought had proven very, very wrong.

Dew met them at the cross path near a stone marked with directional runes. "Good eve, friends." Her wide mouth stretched in a smile and she came up beside Viridi, her head barely reaching his elbow. Dew was the smallest dryad elf, but it never slowed her down. She could climb and run faster than most.

As they continued on, Viridi told Dew what had happened as well.

"You know how I feel about your father," Dew said, "but he's right about you. You aren't weak-minded by any means, Viridi. You can put everything to rights once you're ready. I believe in you."

Her trust warmed his heart, but it didn't chase away his worries. Dew was too much of an optimist. She had the audacity to hope that Father had learned from his mistakes. He didn't know how she had forgiven him.

Viridi tried to push away the memories of when human intruders had come close to the island, but they flooded his mind anyway. The humans hadn't even seen their island through the wards, but the king had been afraid of the fire flickering on their decks, of their lanterns and loud voices. And when Father felt fear, he turned it into rage. He had forced Viridi and the royal guards to wade into the ocean and strike down the intruders with tree magic. Viridi recalled the way pine needles had swarmed the ship like wasps, and how tree roots from the jeweltrees, controlled by Viridi himself, had wrapped around the hull and cracked it like a nut. He would never forget the screams from the sailors as they drowned.

Dew gave him a sad smile, and Felix sighed heavily, as if they had a sense of the pressure on Viridi's shoulders.

Felix led them around a turn in the path. A mouse scurried across the ivy-strewn ground. "If that attack during the first part of his reign hadn't happened, I wonder if the king would have been ... more mild in nature."

A ship of pirates had sailed their small dhow through the wards with no problem. They'd had a witch aboard who knew ward magic. The pirates had come ashore during the day while all the dryad elves were asleep in their trees—Viridi too had been fully asleep in one of the many jeweltrees. He'd only been a youngling at the time. The pirates had cut down two of the largest jeweltrees before Viridi woke. The cold fear he'd felt when they'd cut off the trees' life force ... he shuddered. Viridi had awoken the royal guards, five of the strongest dryad elves, and they'd driven the pirates from the island, killing their captain even with the witch throwing spell after spell at them, her mouth twisting in a tongue Viridi didn't understand. Her magic had been a sickly sort of yellow and it had stunk like rot. But then they had gone, forced away, sailing over the waves. For a full cycle of the moon, the witch's magic had hung around the jeweltrees like a fog of poison.

Could that be what is wrong with the jeweltrees?

"The king should have traveled before he had the weight of all the tribes' future on his shoulders," Dew said. "He might have learned to think beyond this island." She'd gone pale around the mouth, twisting a length of ivy around her fingers, a nervous habit. She was fascinating, so different from the rest of their people. She had the same look— pointed ears, skin that shimmered slightly green in the light —but her personality was like that of an outsider. She had traveled a few times with her sister when she was alive, seen more of the world than most dryad elves, considering hardly any of them ever left the island.

It was difficult to leave. They had to get to know a tree before the tree would house them. Viridi had heard it was exhausting.

"You're right, Dew. I wish he would have. And me too. Expanding our circles of thought would surely be a positive move. I hate that Father and so many of our people fear it."

"They think everyone out there is a pirate or a witch determined to cut down the jeweltrees."

Felix murmured agreement.

Dew beamed at Viridi, then dashed into the star-shadowed forest, no doubt to climb. Dew was an adult, but she acted like a child at times. Braver than even the royal guards, she was an enigma and he adored her.

The last time Dew had traveled, it had ended in tragedy. Her sister had brought back a human lover, a willing and curious fellow. But Father hadn't liked the man's ideas about opening the island to visitors. Accusing them of plotting against him, Father had sentenced Dew's sister and her partner to death. One did not tangle with Father and live to tell the tale.

Felix veered closer to Viridi. "Do you think the trouble with the jeweltrees could be related to the fire prophecy?"

Parents told their children the prophecy before they rested in their trees every morning. Council members and leaders recited it at meetings, and as a reminder before important events. The ancient words never left a dryad elf's memory.

A fire ends the dryad's reign. Watch for the fire, oh Thorned One.

Viridi dragged his hand over a jeweltree as they walked. The tree's energy shimmered into his palm and a pale green light danced across his knuckles.

Please, the tree said into his mind.

So puzzling.

"I don't know how it would be related," he said to Felix, picking up his friend's question again, "but I suppose it's possible. I feel like there is something I'm meant to do to set them straight, but they're so wild and strong. I truly don't know."

"But that isn't all that's on your mind, is it?" Felix asked, tilting his head. "It's not just your fated role and the jeweltrees. If you don't want to talk about it, I'll leave you be."

A shiver of anticipation traveled across Viridi's heart. He didn't try to hide his smile. "I have no idea what is approaching us, figuratively or literally, but there's a sensation in me that is undeniable."

"If it makes you smile like that, I'm all for it. It's been too long since you've been happy."

Viridi ran a hand over a cluster of pine needles as they neared the feasting area. "I can't imagine what turn of events would favor me."

"Life can be wonderfully thrilling," Felix said. "Especially when one has a potential mate..."

Viridi frowned. "Do you have a prospect? Have you felt the lure?"

"No. I thought maybe you had and that's what this was all about."

Viridi shook his head. "I haven't even seen another dryad beyond our tribe and this lot we're spending time with tonight. I need to travel to the other tribes again soon."

But of course, he couldn't. This was all fanciful dreaming. Flexing his dangerous fingers, he swallowed the bitter taste on his tongue.

Felix gripped his upper arm, concern flashing through his gaze. "You can still hope for love, Viridi. Don't stop hoping."

Dew dropped out of a tree and both of them gasped. Hanging by her legs, her leaf-tunic rumpling, she laughed.

"How do you travel through the trees like that?" Viridi was very glad she'd interrupted the conversation. "I feel like I should know how."

"It's not just princes and kings who make the trees sing," Dew said in her melodic voice. "This is where I leave you. Have a mug of something spicy for me!"

In a shuffle of leaves, she was gone.

"I wish she'd feast with us. Just once. I bet she'd enjoy it." Felix studied a cut on his palm, evidence of the growing work they'd been doing in the east. It was a difficult magic by itself and when one combined that with manual labor, it was surprising Felix was even up to enjoying tonight's festivities.

"I've tried to talk her into it, but it's no good," Viridi said, a heaviness settling over his chest. It made sense that Dew wanted nothing to do with being in Father's presence, but that fact alienated her.

In three circles around the feasting area, dryad fires flickered a bright green. Rom had his lyre out and was spilling music into the night, his fingers so incredibly fast. Wearing their finest pine branch coronets, the women danced in pairs. They wove through a ring of men with oaken circlets. It was the summer binding dance, a tradition that helped the tribe bond. Members of the Longleaves tribe had joined in due to the growing project on the eastern shore. The two tribes, both sworn to Prince Viridi and his father the king, had been working hard to repair damage to the island due to the torrential rains they'd had last moon.

Father strode into the green glow of the dryad fires. "Ah. Our star-blessed prince arrives."

Viridi sighed. "Father, greetings." He bowed his head submissively.

Father embraced him roughly, then gave Felix a tight smile. Viridi knew Father was envious of the closeness between Viridi and Felix. "I have a gift for you, my son. A gift worthy of the Thorned One."

The others gathered around, their voices going quiet and their eyes on Viridi as unease spread over his body like a winter's chill.

Father's surprises were never pleasant and always public.

Extending a hand, Father raised his voice. "We have a new arrival to our lands here on the western coast."

A young woman with amethyst eyes walked out of the shadows. She moved gracefully, the dryad power in her obvious from the way the leaves shuffled at her passing.

"I think Helena would make a wonderful companion for you this night, Prince Viridi," Father said.

Viridi's chest tightened, but it had nothing to do with the young girl. She was hardly more than a youngling, and the thought of what Father might have said to her about Viridi's need for a mate summoned a roaring anger inside him. She and her family would have expectations now, expectations he would have to shatter.

But he didn't want to scare or further embarrass the girl, so he bowed respectfully and gave her a smile. She curtseyed, sending a shimmer of emerald magic toward him in a strong display of fealty. He took her arm, and before Father could make even more of a spectacle, escorted her away from the crowd and toward the farthest dryad fire circle.

"I am pleased to spend this feasting time with you," he said, giving her a cup of whatever the servants were handing out on trays. "But I must be honest right away to spare us both from further pain. I do not feel a mating bond with you or anyone here. I never have. I apologize for my father and his ... misplaced enthusiasm."

She drank her mug down and looked around nervously. "I am sorry for any trouble, my prince."

"It's not your fault, and it's no trouble anyway. Would you like to dance?"

She grinned prettily, and the anger toward his father flared again as he took her hand and led her through the simple steps of the Moon Dance, a tradition they all learned as younglings.

Felix trotted over and joined in with a group of three others, lightening the mood nicely.

Across the flickering light of the fires, Father watched them very closely.

Tension bunched the muscles around Viridi's shoulders. He tore his gaze away to focus on his friends. He couldn't control Father. The king reigned in full. But as Viridi's power grew, he would be able to sway Father. Hopefully, he would know what to do when the time came and fate rapped hard on his door.

CHAPTER 3
ISA

Isa hoisted the water bucket higher onto her arm and passed Seigneur and Dame Brune as they talked at the helm.

"I will tie him to a rope and have him swim down to the wreckage," Seigneur was saying to Dame.

Dame's smile curdled the scant amount of oatmeal in Isa's stomach. "He can swim," Dame said. "I have seen it. But what if he isn't able to swim deep enough to reach it?"

Seigneur cocked his head. "We'll tie weights to him."

They were talking about using Nico to ... to do what? To leap into these shark-infested waters to look for some treasure in a submerged ship? How could they so carelessly discuss sending a boy on a potentially deadly mission just for treasure? She gripped the bucket's handle to keep from going for their throats.

"When?" the question was out of her mouth before she could think on it.

They stared at her, and a shiver of fear rattled her bones.

Seigneur fisted his hand, his glove the color of blood. "When we locate Eastern Fang Reef."

Dame, glaring, said, "Get back to work."

Nico would survive. She would offer to swim with him. She'd spent time in the river in the hills beyond Nid de Lapin and she'd ventured into the shallow ocean waters off the coast on one of several family trips during her childhood. She would help Nico. Somehow.

She prayed the Source would give her the patience not to murder someone and would gift her the fortitude to help Nico.

They had one more month of this indenture. She could do this. They could do this.

Just one more moon cycle and both she and Nico would be free.

She hurried to Seigneur and Dame's cabin, a gull crying overhead as she disappeared into the dim to make sure the room was tidy. Unfortunately, several large pools of honey glistened on the floor. Nico must have spilled some honey when he'd carried the tray here for luncheon. He wasn't clumsy. He was just young. On hands and knees, skirt tied up at her thigh, she scrubbed and hummed the tune her mother had once sang to her. It was a song about legends and magic, about sleeping power and possibilities as far and wide as the blue sky.

Ursane popped into the room, grabbing a post to keep herself upright. "Get that cleaned up before they come back, or I'll tell Seigneur about the boy's curse mark."

Isa shivered, then coughed trying to hide her fear. "It's only a bit of honey," she bit out.

Ursane smacked the back of Isa's head and pain lanced through her skull. Fighting back the urge to strike out, Isa set her jaw and suffered as her ears rang. She glared at Ursane.

"Maybe if you'd refrain from beating Nico senseless, he'd be more help to you," Isa said.

Hatred for this woman and the Brunes was a weight on Isa's back, a splinter in her eye, a fire in the deepest corner of her heart.

Her comment earned her another hit to the back of the head.

"If he weren't signed to Seigneur, I'd have left him in Khem," Ursane whispered. "You had better hope they decide he's worth it before we dock again." Her boots sounded smartly against the planking, and then she was gone. The silence hummed in Isa's injured head, and tears seared the edges of her eyes.

A more delicate set of boots clicked down the passage outside the doorway.

Isa scrambled to her feet. "Dame Brune!"

Dame whirled, her well-tailored dress wrapping her legs. She wore a low-slung belt as most highborns did these days in Wylfenden, Balaur, and Lore. "What?" The woman's thick eyebrows drew together tightly. She put her hands on her wide hips.

"Where does Seigneur plan to dock when Nico's and my indenture is up?" Isa asked. "It's less than a month until our release." Then she and Nico could start down their own path. They would use their skills to carve their way in the world.

A gleam passed over Dame's eyes and her lips turned up at one corner. She crossed her arms, leaning against the wall as the ship listed and the lantern above swayed. Source save her, but Isa was simply dying to punch her square in the nose. "Only a month left, hmm?" Dame said. "I don't think you tallied that correctly."

Isa's face grew hot, and she gripped her scrub brush more tightly. "Oh, I did. I tallied every single day at the tapestry workshop." Before the place had burned to the ground and life had gone from pleasantly dull to terrifyingly horrible. "I'm quite good at tallying."

Dame snorted and smoothed the scarlet feather pinned to her headdress. "Your job is buckets and brushes, little mouse. It's not your responsibility to keep track of your indenture. I believe your time with us won't be up until at least three more months. After all, Nico had that fever and we used expensive medicinals on him. You must repay that since you have quite obviously claimed him as your ward in the way that some lowborns do." She fluttered her eyelashes and smiled.

Isa's stomach rolled and she put a hand on the wall. "No … Nico can't take another three months of this…" She was muttering, and Dame wasn't even listening. Isa's thoughts buzzed like angry bees.

Dame started to walk away.

Isa snatched Dame's arm, heat rising in her cheeks and a

crackling feeling spreading from her scalp down into her arms. "You can't treat us like this."

Dame jerked free, her eyes nearly popping from their sockets. She stared down at her sleeve where Isa's fingers had been.

Black marks in exactly the shape of Isa's hand marred the fine fabric.

CHAPTER 4
ISA

Blinking, Isa stumbled back. "I..."

Lightning washed the darkness outside the window at the end of the passage, and thunder rumbled, a sudden storm rising.

Dame stared at Isa, her beady-eyes scratching over her face. Dame whispered something.

"What?" Isa's heart hammered against her ribs.

Had she called her a witch? She went cold all over.

Dame pushed past her and hurried to the stairs leading to the upper deck. As she went, Isa heard Dame whispering a prayer to the Source.

Isa turned her hand over, but there was no ash from the iron grate fires or enough dirt to cause such a complete mark on Dame's clothing. She shook her head. *What just happened?*

She swallowed. Then, watching to make sure Ursane wasn't about to leap from the shadows, she hurried into her and Nico's berth at the bow of the ship. The ship rolled and more lightning flashed through the portholes.

"Nico," Isa hissed into the dark berth.

He coughed and her heart broke. His lungs had never quite recovered from that last ague, and his illness reminded her far too much of the way her parents had died.

"I'm here," he said. "Sorry. I'll get up."

She set a gentle hand on his stomach and kept him lying flat on his poor excuse for bedding—a few rags and a plank of wood set into the ship's wall. "Nah, you don't have any work to do right now. This storm will keep them busy. I just wanted to check on that leg of yours."

"It's not too bad."

Using the flashes of the storm's light to guide her, she pulled the rag he was using as a blanket away from his skinny leg. At nine, he should have been bigger. He had the bones of a far younger child due to lack of food and ongoing illnesses.

"She's broken the skin with that awful stick of hers." Isa forced herself not to collapse under the weight of her impotent rage. "One day I'll put her candle out with that very length of oak, Nico. You watch and see." She knew very well she was full of dung, but it was fun to imagine revenge anyway.

His teeth were white in the dark berth, one missing in the front. "I'll help you."

She ruffled his floppy brown hair and looked into his blue eyes. The color wasn't obvious in the dim room, but in the light, his eyes were the hue of the open sky, and somehow the goodness in him just radiated right through. The curse mark, as Ursane called it, showed just behind Nico's ear. It wasn't scary to Isa; it resembled a tiny rose and was just a birthmark with no magical connotations, good or bad. Plenty of people had them.

"I know you will." She knelt beside him, tucking her threadbare dress under her legs to chase off the cold of the ship's belly. "Very, very soon, our indenture will be up and we'll sail away for our own adventures."

"Where will we sail?"

This was their favorite thing to do at night—to imagine what they might do when they were free. Dame's sharp words echoed through Isa's mind, but she shook them off. She'd find a way to get them off this boat at the next docking. She'd make a break for it and they'd find some small jobs and save up...

"To the island of the dryad elves," she said finally, "where fruit falls right into your lap upon arrival. It tastes like—"

"Like chocolate!"

Isa grinned. "Exactly. And the weather will be so fine that we'll sleep under the stars. Every wish we make will come true."

Nico stared at the top of the berth, his smile wide in the storm's intermittent light and his dimples showing. "So many stars."

"So many wishes. If you believe the old map in Seigneur's cabin, we are close to the dryad elves' island. What would you wish for first?"

He turned onto his side, wincing slightly. His leg had to pain him terribly and the rolling the ship had been doing the last hours wasn't making things easier.

Pushing the image of the black fingermarks on Dame's dress to the back of her mind, she took a deeper breath and settled in to listen.

Nico looked left and right, the lightning reflecting in his big eyes. "I'd wish for a dog."

This was a new one. "What made you think of that?"

"Do you remember when we were in Khem, at the trader's dock?"

How could she forget? The Brunes had stopped there for supplies shortly after leaving Wylfenden, their home kingdom. Two down-on-their-luck thieves had attempted to steal everything from belowdecks while the Brunes were at the market. Since the criminals had simply been hungry and hardly more than boys, Isa and Nico had put up enough of a fight to put them off their mission, sending them away with a serving of flatbread.

"Of course. I don't remember any dogs though."

"There was a spotted one on shore. I saw him through the porthole before the thieves attacked," he said. She'd never stop being amazed by his ability to shove away the bad and enjoy the good in their awful life. "A lady with a big..." He snickered.

"Nico. Behave."

"Shoulder pack. I was going to say shoulder pack."

Isa poked him playfully. "Sure you were."

"The dog had a ball she threw for him. He fetched it as they walked past the docks."

"A dog, then. Second wish?"

The ship lurched forward and Isa just barely caught Nico as he was thrown from his bed. A great crack sounded and a scream pierced the thunder's drumming. They hadn't had a storm like this during their indenture. Though many said this run of the ocean was highly dangerous, so far they'd been lucky. Well, lucky in weather, not lucky in anything else.

Isa tucked him back in and handed him the rope she kept tied to the brass ring on the wall. "Stay here."

"No. Isa!"

His voice faded under the storm's riotous noise and the shouting on the upper deck. Isa grabbed her hem and ran up the stairs. Lightning exploded across the night sky. Seigneur Brune was shouting orders to the crew while Dame Brune held tight to the side of the ship. Waves crested high and crashed over the deck, soaking Isa's flimsy shoes.

"Witch." Dame thrust herself forward, grabbing Isa's arms with pinching fingers. The soaked feather from her fancy headdress fell over one side of her slim, pale face. They nearly fell to the deck as another wave rocked the ship. "This is all your fault. You're cursed, and that boy too. Ursane told me about his mark." Dame whirled around to shout at her husband. "We must throw her over. It's her foul magic that's causing this." She extended her arm, showing the black finger marks.

Isa pulled away. "Or it could be that your husband chose to sail the most dangerous stretch of water in the known world in search of treasure he doesn't need and it's finally catching up to him."

Dame grabbed her again and lashed nails across her face. Hot blood streamed down Isa's chin and throat. Rain beat down and washed it into her dress, its chill numbing the pain of her beatings.

Nico hobbled out of the stairwell. "Leave her alone!"

"Nico, go back down." Isa wanted to pry Dame's hand from her arm, but Dame might do worse if Isa kept antagonizing her. Instead, she looked at Nico pleadingly.

Thunder rocked the very boards of the ship and everyone lost their footing—sailors and nobles alike. Lightning washed the tied-down sails and the mast in blinding white. The roll of the deck tore Dame from Isa.

"Get below!" Seigneur waved at Dame and Ursane, who was grasping desperately to a lashed barrel.

Dame's head twisted and her gaze locked on Nico, who was frowning and wiping his eyes. The ship listed and he fell against the stairwell archway. Blood ran down his ear. Dame crawled to him as the ship groaned. Seigneur shouted orders that sounded more like pleas for help. The sailors worked to pull down the sails, shouting and oblivious to the drama unfolding.

Dame gripped Nico's arm and hoisted him to his feet.

Isa saw red.

She ran, slipping on the wet decking and banging her knee hard. Gritting her teeth, she struggled to her feet.

"Get your hands off him."

Ursane launched herself at Isa and grabbed the back of her dress. Ursane shoved Isa down, then produced a dagger. Ursane put the dagger to Isa's throat. The steel bit at the skin below her jaw.

Dame's grin was disgusting. She dragged Nico a step closer. "You're both cursed. I'm not about to die for a couple of lazy, lackwit servants." She pulled Nico to the side of the ship. The storm growled and the sky split with two quick bursts of lightning.

Isa froze. "Stop."

She wouldn't...

The ship slid sideways.

Dame threw Nico into the sea.

CHAPTER 5
ISA

Isa's whole heart flung itself over with Nico's body. Her scream became a growl and she tore away from Ursane, not feeling the cut of the dagger if there was one, and she leapt from the ship.

She dove into wild waves, then came up with her mouth half full of salty water. "Nico! Nico, I'm here!"

The thunder ate her shouts and the sea pulled her under.

Salt water stung her eyes as she searched the dark water below for any sign of him. But there was only the green-black of the tumultuous ocean and the flash of the storm breaking through the surface. She kicked and rose up, swimming hard to keep her head high enough for a quick breath for her burning lungs. The ship disappeared behind a wall of water.

Shouts and shrieking lanced through the howling winds. "Nico!"

A small hand shot upward through the black waves.

Source, save us. Isa struck out with her arms and kicked as hard as she could. One shoe slipped from her foot as her dress tugged at her like rough hands.

"Isa?" Nico's voice was a light in the dark.

She swam, not feeling anything but a blazing hope. He would live. He had to.

Debris twisted past her on a foaming swirl—a sun-bleached log, a cracked barrel, a length of light green wood.

It was one of Seigneur's pinnaces!

Isa snatched the edge of the lightweight craft and hoisted it upward. The small boat crashed back down. She lurched backward.

Nico's shout grew distant.

Her throat closed. She swam away from the pinnace, shouting Nico's name. "I'm coming." She kicked and kicked and kicked. "Wave your hand."

Thunder drummed, cutting off her words and striking her ears.

Nico's face appeared between the waves, his mouth open and his eyes screwed shut.

She sliced through the water, a new energy rising in her blood, until she had his arm in her grip. His skin was ice. Pulling his arm over her shoulder, she maneuvered him onto her back.

"Hold on to my neck."

He didn't respond, but his chest rose and fell against her.

"Nico!"

With his cold arms draped over her shoulders and his sharp forearms freezing on the sides of her neck, she swam. She had to get to the pinnace. Or somewhere. Already her kicks were weak and her arms were jellied fruit.

"Hold on, my little hope. Hold on."

He murmured something, but the storm raged on, the rain shooting across the waves and piercing like arrows.

The Brunes' ship bobbed over a wave. The main mast lay broken across the deck and a rope flew behind the craft like a tail. She couldn't see any people aboard. Another swell blocked her view, and then she glimpsed the pinnace.

Hung up on a slick, black rock, it rocked violently up and down as she swam toward it. She tried to grasp the edge of the upside-down boat, but it lurched away.

"Hold tightly now, Nico."

She kicked with everything she had left and grabbed hold. Bracing herself on the pinnace and pushing it as best she could against the line of rocks, she nudged Nico's head with her own, rousing him.

"Climb on. Hurry! Nico, now."

The lightning snapped and thunder rolled, farther away now. Rain pelted her hands and cheeks. Her fingers were numb. Nico worked his way over her bowed head and onto the pinnace. He cried out as the boat shifted; she caught him and pushed him up by the leg so that he didn't fall back into the water. The rain relented a bit, and she dragged her weary self onto the upturned boat beside Nico.

They clung to one another, gasping.

Isa ignored the last thrashings of the storm, the ocean's

angry waves, and focused only on the sweet, familiar scent of Nico's hair, which was far preferable to the brine of the sea. She wrapped his small body in her arms and tears seared her cheeks.

WHEN ISA REGAINED HER SENSES AFTER WHAT MIGHT have been unconsciousness or sleep, the sun reflected off a stretch of sand not ten feet from their resting place—the gnarled rock surrounded by shallow and lapping water. The tide must have been responsible for the fact that they were now on land.

Soaked all the way through, she was seated against the black rock. Nico lay across her lap, his face bone-white.

"Nico." She shook him gently, but he didn't stir.

Swallowing, she put a finger in front of his open mouth. Warm breath touched her skin and she sank back, exhaling. Despite her shaking arms and legs, she managed to gather him up and carry him across the mucky expanse where the tide had revealed ground all the way to the bright sand. It felt like a momentous journey.

Collapsing onto the beach, she tried to remember to simply stay alive.

Darkness took her.

SHE WOKE AGAIN ONLY TO FIND NICO SITTING UP, hugging his knees beside her. His gaze was on the sky. The sun had fallen fully, and night reigned.

Groaning at the multitudes of aches and pains in her body, Isa rolled onto her back. Stars glittered in the widest, blackest sky imaginable. Her limbs were light—too light—and she reached for Nico's hand, taking his fingers in hers. They were both so, so cold even though the night breeze was mild across Isa's cheeks.

"My wish came true," Nico said, his voice torn and thin.

She felt as though she were dreaming. "What was your wish?"

"That you weren't dead."

Isa squeezed his hand. "Thanks for that."

He chuckled. "You're welcome."

Sitting up, she gathered him into her arms and tried to will her warmth into his bony frame. "We're both alive." She said it to make sure it was true. Her head was filled with seawater and fear. The sand crunched between her bare toes. When had she lost her shoes and stockings?

A branch snapped behind them. Nico broke away and stood, his eyes wide.

Isa turned to see a dark forest limned in starlight. And then...

The stars glowed over the silhouette of a tall, slender man with tousled dark hair and a proud nose. She squinted to see him better as the trees seemed to lean toward him, the leaves shuffling.

A warmth gathered around her heart and she gasped, suddenly unable to breathe easily. It was as if the stranger had grabbed hold of her very soul with a gentle but demanding hand and her body and mind had no choice but to follow in its wake.

Suddenly, soft leaves wrapped her body. Willowy branches tangled around her waist and thighs. Strong arms held her fast. It was a storm of sensations, of touches and murmurs, of heat and the ache of longing. She couldn't make sense of it, but she couldn't say it was unpleasant. Quite the opposite. The taste of flower nectar touched the tip of her tongue as the stranger whispered in her ear, breath hot ...

But he was no stranger. She knew him. But how?

He was twenty years old and loved watching the moon rise on summer nights. The stranger who wasn't a stranger delighted in the loyalty of his friends. She could almost see their faces in his memories. The stranger's arms around her felt like coming home and she smiled and leaned into him. He told her the name of every tree on the island. This moment was a thousand moments. He gazed at her lovingly, then his eyes went hot with desire and a grin tugged at her lips. His look turned feral, demanding something she couldn't understand. The cool earth pressed against her back and branches lashed her wrists together and pulled her arms over her head. A soft kiss heated the base of her throat and she gasped—

And she was back on the beach beside Nico like she'd had a waking dream.

The man in the forest had disappeared.

CHAPTER 6
VIRIDI

Viridi stumbled back a step, feeling as though the stars themselves had fallen to the earth to live inside his chest and illuminate him from the inside. He put a hand to his pounding heart and swallowed, his throat gone dry at the sight of her.

This was what he'd been feeling, the event that had drawn him to the coastline time and time again in the last sennight, the fated occurrence that had danced at the edge of his dreams, always out of reach.

This was the moment.

Her arrival.

She was all he could see, scent, and feel. He inhaled and shuddered with pleasure at the simple fact that she was here on his island. What did this mean for him, for the Thorned One?

Take her, the trees whispered. *She is your mate.*

And for once, he was of the same mind as the cursed trees.

CHAPTER 7
ISA

She took a shuddering breath. "Did you see that?" Her heart tapped madly against her ribs and she stood, putting Nico behind her.

"The man? Yes."

Night insects trilled, and the breeze danced in the thick clusters of tiny leaves.

From the sea, a voice called out. "Ahoy! Anyone there?" They spoke in the common tongue, language of the kingdom of Lore.

Nico launched himself down the beach. "Look! Another ship." His feet—one shoed and the other bare—threw sand as he hurried toward a skiff that was coming ashore.

A ship almost as large as the Brunes' bobbed in the silvery waves beyond the shallows. Torches flickered at one end of the craft, and Isa thought she saw crew moving about.

Sweat beading on her upper lip, she took off after Nico.

These could be pirates, slavers—anyone. They might even be worse than Ursane and the Brunes.

"Nico, come back!"

A woman wearing trousers leapt from the skiff onto the sand, a hand raised in greeting. The man who pulled the skiff in smiled widely, his teeth white in the low light.

He had pointed ears and horns.

"Fae."

Isa hated that she was immediately distrustful, but she'd never interacted with a fae and most said they were incredibly clever and could be very cruel.

Catching up to Nico, she grabbed the back of his ripped tunic and flung him behind her.

What was a fae doing this far from Lore? They weren't even close to the trading island of Khem anymore, were they? Had these folk been following the Brunes in order to steal their stash of provisions and coin?

Nico tugged her sleeve and looked at her with those big eyes that melted her soul. "Princess Brielle has a fae friend, so fae must be good, right?"

"The princess is a politician," Isa said. "She would befriend anyone just to help Wylfenden."

The fae bowed low, sweeping a hand through the air dramatically. He straightened and a spark lit his eyes, a glint of mischief not unlike the one Nico had when she'd caught him sneaking into the ship's kitchen last week. "This is my lovely wife," the fae said. "How can we be of service?"

The woman took a small apple from her cloak pocket

and held it out to Nico. "Are you hungry, love? Please take this."

Nico reached for it, but Isa pushed him back gently.

"Thank you, but no," she said. "How did you find us here?"

"We saw the wreckage." The fae glanced toward the sea. "Any other survivors?"

"I ... I don't think so," Isa said. She tried not to be happy about people dying, but she failed miserably. They'd done their best to kill her and Nico. The sea could have them with her best wishes. Hope was a wind filling the sails of her heart.

The fae bent his head and whispered something melodious in the fae tongue, a few phrases that might have been a prayer for the dead. It sounded reverent.

Isa tried to feel guilty again, but she couldn't manage it. Fatigue stripped her of any artifice.

"We can take you to a port if you like?" the woman said, tucking a strand of dark hair behind her ear. "I can't imagine you wish to stay here after all the stories our men have told us about the vicious dryad elves."

The fae spun in a circle, arms extended and a smile creating dimples in his handsome face. "Well, it is rather gorgeous, isn't it? How about we explore a bit before heading back to dull civilization?"

Isa held Nico against her and he struggled to step away. "What did you say your names were? And what your purpose is out here in the middle of the ocean?"

"Ah, I am Captain Shadowhood and this is Merewyn of the Bones, kindly pirates at your service, milady."

"That's what I thought. Nico, run into the forest and don't stop. Find our friend."

"But ... that man, you mean? He's not—"

She whirled and knelt, taking Nico by the arms. "Go." Anything was better than pirates.

He stammered, then ran off, his feet kicking up sand.

Isa set herself between Nico's path and the pirates. "If you plan to take him, you'll have to get through me first." She sounded like a grand fool, because who was she against two people, let alone a fae? But she wasn't going to let Nico be taken without a fight. "I won't win, but I won't go down easy either." Her voice shook so hard she thought maybe they wouldn't even understand her roughly accented Lore.

The woman held out her hands. "Eh, now, love. Calm yourself. We're not slavers. We only steal from the rich to give to the poor."

"Likely story."

The fae stared in the direction Nico had gone. "I'm just disappointed they've never heard of me."

The woman shook her head at her fae husband. "Focus, Werian."

Isa jerked in surprise. "Werian? I thought you said your name was Shadowhood?" She swallowed, her heart thudding in her ears. What were these two playing at?

"Yes, wife, I thought my name was Shadowhood."

"If we're going to gain their trust, we need to share our

true identities," the woman said to the fae. Then she faced Isa. "I'm Princess Rhianne of the Agate Court."

"You're the witch who married the fae prince? Wait." She faced Werian. "You're the fae prince. I ... I don't know what to say..." Isa's thoughts tangled into knots.

The witch woman—Princess Rhianne—nodded. "So we aren't going to harm you. We have everything we need, and from the stories about us, surely you know we aren't that horrible."

She had indeed heard stories about the fae prince and his human witch wife, that they traveled extensively throughout the world and were the life of the party at every court they visited, including Wylfenden's. They had false names and glamours they used when it pleased them, or so the tales claimed. Rhianne and Werian were most likely good folk.

And Nico was running from them and toward the unknown.

"Nico!"

CHAPTER 8
ISA

Sweat rolled down Isa's back. She clutched at her tattered dress as she sped toward the forest. They had a better chance with these royals than they did with whatever wild animals or strange men lived in the woods on this seemingly deserted island. "Nico, come back!"

"We'll find him." Fae Prince Werian sped past her and into the trees.

Rhianne stayed with Isa as they hurried away from the beach and into the forest.

Isa pushed through the brush, fatigue tugging hard at her limbs as Rhianne took a wand from the back of her belt and thrust it upward. She said something very fast in the Lore language and light shot from the wand and into the air. Tiny globes of amethyst and gold light illuminated the trunks and branches of the trees as they all worked their way along an animal path.

"Nico, it's safe. Where are you?"

Vines with hand-sized white flowers blocked the view farther down the path. He could be anywhere in this lush forest. Ferns brushed Isa's dress as she walked as quickly as possible. Her legs trembled and she stumbled. Princess Rhianne helped her up with a gentle smile.

"I'm Isa, by the way. What do you know about this place?" Isa looked left and right, her blood sluicing through her veins like chips of ice. Her body wasn't going to let her stay conscious for much longer.

"First off, I don't see how we broke through the wards," Rhianne said. "The storm, I suppose? I most likely know the same stories as you do about the dryad elves, if that is indeed where we are. The dryad elves can snap ships in two with trees they control. They hate intruders. Not exactly the sort you want to invite over for tea."

They found Werian stopped at a large tree with pale bark that flaked like croissant layers. Once they'd caught up, Werian pointed a finger toward the canopy.

He looked into the branches, his horns almost invisible in the dim and the tangle of his dark hair. "Good sir, please climb down. I promise only to eat one of your arms. You'll be just fine."

Rhianne smacked him. "You're safe with us, as is Isa," she called up. "I'm only supposing he is your brother," she said to Isa.

"I've taken him under my wing, so to speak. We aren't kin, but I feel like we are. Nico," she called up into the tree, feeling oddly bashful about voicing her emotions. "I can't quite see you, but if you're there, follow his directions. He is the fae prince of the Agate Court. The one you mentioned."

"Ah. So *he* has heard of me," Werian said.

Rhianne pinched the bridge of her nose.

"You mean Princess Brielle's friend?" Nico's thready voice moved through the tree's branches.

Isa sighed. Thank the Source and the Goddess Vahly he was alive. "Yes. Now, come down. Use those strong muscles of yours and take your time." He had to be nearly falling over with fatigue.

Nico appeared, his feet finding a branch while his hands gripped another.

"May I?" Werian approached Isa, getting closer to the tree's trunk.

Oh. She'd forgotten—fae could heal. "Of course. Thank you."

Werian took Nico under the arms and set him carefully on the ground. Then the fae set one hand on Nico's chest and shut his eyes.

Nico's eyes were wide as saucers. "Is this magic?"

"It is." Werian winked at him.

Nico looked to Isa and she thought her heart might snap with joy. "It feels so nice and warm." He blinked and yawned as Werian stepped back.

"Time for a nice sleep now, lad." Werian glanced at Isa. "Your turn, if you like?"

"Go on," Rhianne urged her. "If we're to figure out the

mystery of this island of potential wishes or possible death, you'll need your strength."

Isa swallowed and turned toward Werian. He placed his hand on her shoulder. Warmth flooded her body. The cuts on her face and neck prickled with heat as they mended. The lump on her head dwindled to nothing, and the dragging tiredness inside her bones dissipated. She was still hungry, but by the time Werian finished, she felt better than she had since taking up with the Brunes.

Rhianne scooped up Nico, who didn't argue and instead set his head against her shoulder.

"Thank you so much." Tears blurred Isa's vision. It had been ages since someone had cared for her. Even though she'd heard of Werian and Rhianne, they were strangers, and Isa probably should have kept her distance. But she was too worn out to fight at this point.

"Let's make camp." Werian started back toward the beach. "I think I have some food in the skiff, and I can call some of the crew on shore to bring us some drink."

"Halt, intruders," a voice called out.

Isa whirled around. A dozen men walked out of the deep forest, spears aimed and ready.

"On your knees, intruders." A man with braided, moon-white hair stepped forward. Fingers of starlight touched the tips of his pointed ears.

Isa froze. Seigneur's map had been accurate. *They're dryad elves.*

Nico's mouth hung open as much as hers did.

The warriors were dressed in armor crafted from gold, bronze, and dark green leaves that had somehow been fashioned into tunics and belts, trousers and boots. They had large knives on their woven belts, and small vines with bright green leaves twined through their hair. Isa's mind went from afraid to fascinated and back again.

Werian rubbed his hands together like he was somehow enjoying this. "Ooo, are you elves like the Balaur and Shadow elves? Was I right in guessing this is the dryad elf island? I had no idea you were truly real."

Nico grinned from ear to ear.

The elven man set his spear against Werian's throat. "On. Your. Knees."

"Of course. So sorry to alarm you." Werian went to his knees. "We are peaceful sorts. There's no need for violence." His gaze flitted to Rhianne and Isa.

He probably was considering whether or not he and his witch wife could take this group of elves. And possibly whether or not to tell these folk who they were. Would these elves even know about royalty and armies and what might happen if you angered one?

Isa just hoped Werian would continue to be peaceful. If it came to a fight, she and Nico would most likely end up on the end of one of those spears. She knew how to use a knife and do a few strikes and blocks—Father had taught her—but it would be nothing against this group.

Maybe if she simply explained...

"My ship wrecked," she said. "I didn't plan to come here and bother you." She stuck with the Lore tongue since it was the trade language that most knew and the elf had used it already. "We're happy to leave with these two at your earliest convenience."

Werian chuckled. "Earliest convenience."

The elf guarding Rhianne pointed at her waist. "Give me your wand, witch."

Werian's face darkened, the starlight sliding past his narrowed eyes. "Eh, now, good sir. If you like that finger you're pointing, stay away from my wife."

The elf huffed a laugh. "You believe you can defeat and dismember me?"

"Possibly, but my wife *definitely* can."

Isa grinned.

Rhianne slowly set Nico down and he ran to Isa. The elves didn't aim for Nico, but they did stiffen at the sudden movement.

Nico knelt beside her and wrapped one arm tightly around her waist. "Are they the ones from the story?" he whispered, his light eyes trained on the leader. "Is the one we saw here somewhere?"

"They might be the dryad elves. I don't know. But I don't think the one we saw is here. He had dark, wavy hair."

"Where's the elf who spied on us?" Nico said before Isa could put a hand over his mouth. "The one with the dark hair and the scary eyes?"

"Kid," she hissed, her stomach clenching with fear. He was going to get himself killed. "Please, Nico." She wished he knew how to stay quiet. Not that she'd been good at teaching him that particular skill.

Ignoring Nico's question and her outburst, the elves collected Werian's sword and dagger, as well as Rhianne's wand and sword.

The elf who seemed to be their leader gestured to two others and said something in a language full of rolling vowel sounds and odd clicks, then he faced Isa and the rest.

"Follow us," he said. "Run, and we will end your lives as soon as you turn your back."

Werian and Rhianne traded a look, then the fae shrugged. They stood and began to do as ordered.

What choice was there? Unless Werian could signal his

crew, they were outnumbered. And as soon as the rest of these strange elves knew they were here, those odds would grow even worse. Maybe they would stop for sleep and Isa could manage an escape with Nico. Surely, these guards would care more about securing their hold on a fae and a witch than two humans, one of whom was a small boy. She didn't want Werian and Rhianne to be hurt, but if it came to a choice between Nico's life and theirs, she knew exactly what she would choose.

The forest thickened as they trudged onward. The melon-hued light of dawn passed through wide branches of flickering leaves and illuminated silver dew drops on the ferns and thick mosses lining the path. The scents of sea salt and freshly blooming flowers danced through the breeze. Isa's fear faded in the face of such beauty.

Nico stumbled and Isa lifted him, trying to carry him. But he gently pushed away and attempted to begin walking again. "I'm too big for you to carry. I'll be all right."

The elven leader glanced backward at them, his eyes narrowing. He cut a look at the fellow beside him.

The second elf turned and squatted. He touched his shoulder. "You may ride on my back if you wish, youngling."

Rhianne moved toward Nico. "I can take him."

"Thank you." Isa much preferred Rhianne holding Nico than these violent strangers.

"I'm all right." Nico jogged a few steps, catching up with the leader. "Stop coddling me."

Isa blew out a breath and prayed the goddesses would watch over him. "As you wish," she said tightly.

The leader looked down at Nico and nodded once as if approving. Nico glared back. Isa longed to snatch him back to keep him away from these elves, but she shook her head, smiling ruefully. She couldn't help but be proud of him for that courageous glare.

They walked for ages, the sun rising fully and casting a glowing light onto the tree seeds floating through the air. The path opened up to show a village of wooden homes, larger than some on High Street in Nid de Lapin or in Khem. Each appeared to be grown from the very trees nearby. At the end of the main thoroughfare, a ring of trees —each one as wide as ten men—towered over the village's outskirts.

The elves brought them toward a line of elven warriors guarding an individual seated on a chair made of twisted branches that reached high.

The fellow on the—well, she supposed it was a throne of sorts—looked up from a large leaf he'd been studying. In his fair hair he wore a crown of vines threaded with scarlet leaves.

"I thought I sensed new souls on our land." Lines stretched from the sides of his eyes, showing age, but he stood quickly and was certainly not too old to be a physical threat, not to mention his impressive array of warriors. "How did you manage to break through our wards?"

"You are the dryad elves." Nico leapt forward, his mistrust for them fading in his obvious excitement.

"Please forgive his youthful exuberance, Your ...

Majesty," Isa said, trying to keep her voice calm and steady. She had no idea what to call a dryad elf king.

Isa held her breath as Rhianne shifted, her hand going where her wand had been on her belt. Werian growled, a barely audible sound that raised the hairs on Isa's neck. Nico bowed his head and clamped his lips shut.

A bit too late, Nico.

Could she throw herself on Nico if this king of sorts decided to punish his outburst? She apologized again.

The king raised his silver eyebrows. "You dare to make requests after invading my land without any invitation?"

"I ... wouldn't you do so if your kin were threatened?"

The warriors eyed their king as he walked a circle around them.

The king's head whipped around. "We are not the same, human. Do not suppose you can bridge the distance between our cultures."

An elven man with tousled dark hair and fierce, deep brown eyes stared at Isa as he walked into the village.

Lightning struck Isa's chest and she inhaled sharply.

It was him.

The one from the beach.

So many of his kind had fair hair and light eyes. He did resemble them in his slender but muscled form and his pointed ears, but something about him, besides his hair color, seemed ... different.

He flexed his hands as he walked forward. The end of every finger ended not in a nail but in a dark and sharpened point. Alarm shot through her. His ears weren't simply pointed elven flesh but were sharp and brown like his fingertips, like his ears turned into branches as they tapered and disappeared into his messy hair.

As he approached the king, who watched him warily, the roots of the large trees shifted just slightly—so subtly that she wasn't certain she'd even seen it happen. A column of the morning sun broke through the canopy and touched his forearm. His skin glowed a soft green before fading into its original shade once more.

What is he?

Focusing on his father, Viridi stalked forward, the trees whispering on the wind.

Watch. See. She is yours to take...

He gritted his teeth as he tried not to stare too long at the beautiful young woman from the shoreline. *Silence,* he said back to the trees.

Yes, they were in agreement that this woman was his fated mate, but they wanted him to drain her energy, to absorb her instead of cherish her. Their whispers grew to a low roar.

Silence, he mentally commanded again.

The trees and their riotous spirits shuffled and howled in his dryad ears, but finally they went quiet.

The woman glowed faintly. No one else would see it; Viridi knew enough of his kind and the way their eyes saw their fated mates. What was he to do with this development? He still wanted Father to persuade everyone to relocate to the Pearl Isles until he untangled the mystery of the jeweltrees and made sure he wasn't a threat. What could he do with the woman? She was in danger here—not only because of Father's hatred of outsiders, but because of the Thorned One he would become.

Father put on the expression that said he didn't want to scare Viridi off. He knew how much he'd angered him at the feasting by proposing that the woman, Helena, could be his mate. Viridi hated that appeasing, cunning look. Viridi wished Felix were here—he was likely still working at the eastern coastline or had already gone to sleep in his tree.

"My son," Father said, "how kind of you to take note of this disturbance. How are you today?" He spoke in the dryad tongue so that the newcomers wouldn't understand.

Father would never in a thousand years stand by while he claimed a human as a mate. Viridi needed time to figure out what to do with that information and how to proceed.

One thing was certain: Viridi wasn't giving her up for Father.

He might release her for other reasons, but not for the wicked king whose seed had sown him.

"I'm doing fine, Father," he bit out. "What do you plan to do to these intruders?"

"You could ask how I am faring, but of course..." Father shook his head in that dramatic way of his, and Viridi had to fight not to look skyward in annoyance. "I plan to imprison them and think on it."

Imprison? His mate? His dark blood raced and his lips parted. "Don't. I am drawn to the young woman," Viridi said, surprising himself. "May I keep her and request royal treatment for her friends?"

The corners of Father's eyes twitched and he crushed the storyleaf in his hand. But then he smoothed his features and lifted his free hand in a gesture of acceptance. "You never ask for a thing, my son. Of course, I will order it done. But what if she won't have you?" His gaze skipped to Viridi's thorned fingertips.

Viridi's heart shuddered at the thought of rejection. If she wouldn't have him, even if they only had a short time, his soul would crack in two. He couldn't look at her; his face might show that very fear. And he didn't want to give Father the satisfaction of reacting to his taunt. Father loved the idea that Viridi might someday be a monster that could forever protect the island, but he was also slightly horrified by him. Father had never been good at hiding his emotions.

"I'll worry about that if it happens," Viridi said, forcing his voice to remain smooth and unruffled by emotion.

Father nodded, and stepped back to allow Viridi to speak to those gathered.

"Welcome to the Isle of Dryads," he said, allowing his deep voice to carry over the whisperings of the boy, the murmuring of the other dryads, and the clatter of the wind in the forest.

The young woman's amber gaze darted around his face and body. Every glance was a press of warm sun, and his lips parted, momentarily lost in what he was going to say next. Her hair fell over one shoulder, tangled and sandy but still beautiful, its hue like the branches of the darkest tree in the forest. She seemed to shine brighter than everyone else and he couldn't tear his eyes away. He found himself walking up to her and taking her callused hand in his. She was so soft, but also so strong. He sensed fatigue in her.

He kissed her wrist and her breath snagged, but she didn't pull away. "What is your name?"

"Isa Bisette, a subject of Wylfenden."

His fingers traced the calluses on her palm and she shivered, her scent telling him she was enjoying his attention. His body warmed, his mind imagining her bare back under his hands. "You have been working too hard, Lady of the Sun."

"You're telling me," she said, a twisting note to her voice.

He grinned. She had spirit. "Well, that part of your life is over."

"Oh, it is? Am I to die and work no more, or do you have a better alternative?" She leaned closer. "The king doesn't seem to like us," she whispered. Her cheeks reddened like perhaps she'd shocked herself with her pluck.

So brave and outspoken, this Lady of the Sun.

Her direct look sent a shot of heat through his body.

"If you'll allow it," he said, "I will take you to my home and treasure you like all should treasure the sun."

"I..." Her cheeks pinked and his heart rose at the idea of making those cheeks even pinker. "So you're not going to kill us? What about Nico?" Her gaze went to the boy beside her.

"The boy will come with us too. I have a large home and

room enough for you, him, and those two if you wish for them to be treated kindly." He gestured at Rhianne and Werian. "Or shall I end them to please you, Lady?"

She shook her head, laughing in what he supposed was surprise. "Please, take care of them too if you will. They have been kind to us and are important figures in the kingdom of Lore."

As much as he didn't want to turn away from her, Viridi stepped toward the other woman and the fae. He bowed slightly. "Greetings, I am Prince Viridi of the dryad elves."

The woman curtseyed and smiled. "I'm Princess Rhianne of the Agate Court, and this is High Prince Werian of the same, son to the Fae Queen."

The fae nodded, bowing respectfully, a glimmer of fae cleverness in his eyes. They would have to keep a watch on that one.

"I wish to bestow my favor on this party of travelers, Father. Will you respect my wishes?" Viridi knew he'd never say no to his potentially monstrous son. There was no future in this endeavor, of course. At some point, the jeweltrees' voices would grow too loud in his ears and the trees would call for their champion. He would have to give up this beauty and the joy of her company. The night would come when he'd wake from his home tree as the most feared and honored creature of the dryad elves, the Thorned One. It was only a matter of time.

Father raised his arms, the leaves of his cloak ruffling in the wind and the morning sun casting his shadow. "These outsiders are deemed our visitors, our guests, by order of the prince. No harm shall come to them and their every demand will be considered."

"Come," Viridi said to Isa, holding out his arm.

"Forgive me for looking a gift horse in the mouth and all of that," Prince Werian said, "but for how long do we have your good graces? Is there a limit to your kind generosity?"

Wise man to ask, Viridi thought.

"As long as you care to remain here ... and as long as the prince wills it," Father said.

Isa took Viridi's arm, and he led her and the rest of her party into the forest. The pines swayed in greeting as they passed and the maples nodded their leafy heads. It was pleasant having her hand on him, her touch light and her walk graceful. Dark circles hung under her lovely amber eyes. She needed healing.

"Prince Werian," he called out over his shoulder. "Perhaps you could lend your healing magic to my lady once we stop."

Werian nodded distractedly. He and his lady wife were watching open-mouthed as the others fell into their trees for the day.

"What ... how does this work?" Rhianne asked as she watched Rom's emerald magic flicker and his body disappear into his walnut tree.

"We dryads sleep all day inside our home trees to gain nourishment. Yes, we still eat in this form at night, but most of our strength comes from the trees, from the sunlight they take in and the nutrients from the earth."

"Why aren't you sleeping?" Isa's gaze flicked to his thorned fingertips.

"As you can tell," he said as the rest of her party caught up, the boy skipping and looking this way and that, "I'm a bit different than the rest."

Isa nodded and took a quick breath, her gaze going to his eyes, then to the tips of his pointed ears. She seemed nervous. He didn't blame her. This had to be a strange and frightening experience. As far as he knew, there were no other dryad elves in the world, so this would be the first and only time she'd seen people like his.

He wondered what she was thinking right now.

CHAPTER 11
ISA

Is he leading us to our deaths?

Surely he wouldn't call her Lady of the Sun and promptly kill her with those wooden talons of his. *Surely.* She swallowed. With his dark eyes and the edge of the wild in him, he was absolutely beautiful. His scent lingered on the air, a blend of nectar and crushed leaves. The memory of that strange magic on the beach colored her mind. She knew him deeply, completely. But it was ridiculous. How could she possibly know him at all? Maybe the event on the shore had been a trick, a spell dryad elves could cast on unsuspecting women.

Nico was staring at Viridi.

"Are you all right?" she mouthed to him.

He grinned widely, his dimples showing as he nodded.

That was all she needed for now. They had escaped the Brunes and hadn't perished in the sea.

"Oooooo," a female voice echoed from the trees near the path.

Viridi looked into the branches of a mossy maple. "Ah, Dew. How are you today?"

Isa followed his gaze and tried to see who was up there.

A branch snapped, leaves shuffled violently, then a person appeared at his feet. It was a short elven woman with her hair gathered into one large knot at the back of her head. She squinted at Isa like she had trouble seeing.

"I am well, and thank you for asking, Prince Viridi," Dew said. "I like speaking in the common tongue like this." Her smile widened as she looked back to Viridi. "Who are your guests?"

"Our ship wrecked," Nico said, not even trying to hide his burning curiosity at seeing such a small person. "Those two," he said, pointing at Prince Werian and Princess Rhianne, "are royalty who just showed up. By accident."

"I like to think we can magically sense when people are in need and we hie to their sides to aid them," Werian said, grinning.

"No, it was all chance," Rhianne said. "But a happy happenstance, I'd say."

Dew laughed loudly. "Yes. You'll be housing them in your keep, Prince?" Dew asked Viridi.

"Indeed." His gaze slid to Isa and the heat in his dark eyes made her blush.

His fingers brushed over her arm, and events that she hadn't experienced flashed through her mind. Viridi running along the beach with Dew and another dryad elf. Viridi holding the hand of a woman. His mother. Somehow, she knew that fact. The love between them fluttered through her own heart and his grief over her loss sang through her soul. She gritted her teeth and tried to drive the images and sounds from her head. What was this strange magic?

"Oh, I see how it is." Dew elbowed Isa roughly, bringing her back to the present. "You enjoy that, my lady." She scanned Isa's torn and poor clothing and confusion flickered over her face. But then that emotion cleared as quickly as a cloud on a windy day, leaving behind that smile again. "Low folk like us should leap at a chance to see what a royal's bed feels like, eh?" She laughed like a tavern wench.

Isa almost wished she were back on the ship. Almost. She coughed to cover her embarrassment. "I wouldn't..."

Viridi seemed unperturbed by Dew and her erroneous guess that Isa and he would be ... well ... he continued down the path, the trees shifting in his presence as if to greet him. They likewise flicked their leaves in pleasure at Werian's appearance too, which made Viridi raise his eyebrows, showing he was impressed by the fae's influence on the forest.

"I would," Dew said, unfortunately taking up the embarrassing conversation once more.

"I'm sorry, but who are you?" Isa asked.

"The hermit." Dew nodded and pulled Isa back a bit. "Give me a moment with your lady, my prince?"

Viridi nodded and walked on. The others, led by Viridi's quick pace, continued and gave them privacy.

Dew stared into Isa's eyes like she was searching for a truth hidden there. "I explore matters of deep spirit."

"As well as pining over the dryad prince's attentions?" she asked, raising an eyebrow.

Dew snorted a laugh. "Pining. Funny. Since we're dryads. I've missed humans. You're so *ridiculous*." The way she said the word made it sound more like a compliment than an insult. "He most likely saved you from his father the king, yes?"

"I suppose he did," Isa said. "The king seemed inclined to imprison us, at the least."

"You don't talk like a servant, but you're dressed like one." Dew grabbed Isa's hand and turned it over, examining her many calluses. "And you have the hands of a servant."

"I was adopted into a tapestry weaver's home. I was taught to tally and to read and write three languages. I'm not ignorant. Not of everything, anyway."

"Well, seems to me you owe the dryad prince a bit of fun."

"Like stars I do."

"I like that Wylfenden accent of yours. Now, calm down, child. You can't tell me he's not alluring." Dew rubbed her hands together and regarded Viridi's backside without even trying to hide her appreciation. She even let out a quiet, low whistle.

"He has talons, or thorns, for fingers," Isa hissed in a whisper, wishing Dew would drop this mad conversation.

But she only wiggled her eyebrows. "Decidedly

monstrous, yes." Then she purred like a big cat and bit her lip.

"You're wild."

"Proud of it. Let yourself be who you may be, child," Dew said as she swung up into the nearest maple.

"You don't look much older than me. Why do you call me child?"

"Because you haven't grown into yourself yet. But you will. You will. And it starts with embracing all that fire you have hiding inside you."

Isa's mouth fell open. "How did you know about—?"

But then Dew was gone, only the rustle of the moving leaves telling her where she climbed, higher and higher into the maple tree.

How did Dew know about Isa accidentally burning a mark in Dame Brune's sleeve?

No, she couldn't know. That was impossible. But then what had she been talking about—*that fire inside?* Did Isa have some disease that only this Dew person could detect, a defect in her flesh? She shook her head. She'd always been too imaginative when it came to illness. Most likely Dew was being metaphorical. The fire inside was only a passion or some such thing.

"Please forgive the bluntness of our hermit," Viridi said as Isa caught up. Viridi led them, his stride long due to his height and his tone easy. "She is a friend." He ran a hand through his hair and sunlight caught his forearm, making the flesh shimmer a subtle green.

They arrived at a towering oak with wide-lobed leaves,

and acorns as big as Isa's fist. The tree grew so that the trunk created an archway of sorts, and moss hung over the passage like a curtained doorway.

Viridi broke away from her, bent his head, and pulled the moss back. "Enter if you wish, Lady of the Sun."

She did so and was rewarded with the view of a tremendous hall. The inside of the oak was hollow, and the tree's massive limbs stretched overhead like hewn beams in a great castle. Soft green light filtered down to scatter across a floor laid out with glittering stones in patterns of roots that curled around lines of writing.

"What do they say?" she asked. This had to be a dream. Everything was so lovely and she was being treated like a queen.

Viridi crouched to get close to the writing, and she did likewise, Nico leaning on her and Werian and Rhianne stopping close by.

"This one," he said, drawing a careful thorned finger across the shining black stones that made up the words, "invites one to shed the day upon arrival, to breathe in the air of this moment."

Nico sighed. "That's nice."

"It is," Isa agreed. She stood and pointed at a phrase written in slightly larger letters. "What about that one? Seems it's set in a place of importance, where everyone can see." The writing went all the way from the base of a curving, wooden-slat staircase to a doorway cloaked in flowering vines.

Viridi's smile warmed her. He was just so incredibly striking. She could stare at him forever.

"It says you are the earth," he said, his deep voice echoing along the smooth walls of the tree castle, "and the earth is you. You are the air and the air is you. Those are the two strongest elements of magic here."

The memory of the singed handprint on Dame's dress, the marking that her own hand had somehow wrought, flashed through Isa's memory. Had that been magic? It was impossible. She had no magic.

"What is it?" Viridi took her hand and traced a slow line along her knuckles.

His touch was divine and drove away her fear with its baffling familiarity. She longed to be honest with him, to ask him about their moment and the borrowed memories, to see if he'd ever seen someone who could scorch with a touch—someone who didn't have a wand and wasn't a witch. But what if she was overreacting? Perhaps it had been ash or dirt on her hands and her feelings about Dame Brune putting off the end of the indenture simply boggled her brains momentarily.

"It's nothing. I'm just tired."

"Of course you are. You've all been through a harrowing experience. I apologize for my fellow dryad elves. They are rather protective of this island."

"Have you been attacked in the past?" Werian asked as Viridi led them through the doorway of flowered vines.

Isa inhaled deeply as she ran her hand lightly over the velvet petals, passing through the decorative barrier. The larger flowers smelled sweet like vanilla, and the smaller ones had a tart scent like cherries.

Behind her, Nico stopped and pulled the vines over his head to make it look like he had hair like a maiden of old. Isa rolled her eyes, but gave him a smile. Yes, this was truly like a dream, like one of their stories.

"We have been attacked, but it's been ages. I suppose we are a people who have long memories," Viridi said.

At the top of the stairs, a wide landing held five dryad elves in dark green tunics and soft-looking trousers made from what appeared to be mushrooms and leaves. In unison, they bowed very low to Viridi.

Were they about to argue against Viridi bringing them here? Isa clutched her ripped clothing and wished Nico would have remained closer to her side instead of peering around Viridi and flitting here and there, looking at everything.

What could she do if this new group of elves attacked?

"Julian and Calva," Viridi said, "please attend to Lady Isa and young Nico."

Julian bowed again, his fair braid dropping over his broad shoulder.

The woman next to him, presumably Calva, bowed and her dark pink lips moved into a quick smile. She had longer, more pointed ears than most of the dryad elves.

Werian cleared his throat quietly and raised a hand. "Please allow me to heal Lady Isa as you suggested, Prince Viridi. I've done so once already, but she needs more attention."

"Of course. Thank you."

Werian set his hand on Isa's shoulder again while Rhianne spoke quietly to Nico about another castle she'd visited in the mountains. The healing magic from the fae prince's hand soothed Isa and she took a deep breath.

"Thank you, Prince Werian, Princess Rhianne," she said.

They gave her a nod each.

"Lady Isa," Werian whispered. "Are you fully human? Forgive the intrusion, but your energy feels … different somehow."

What did he mean? "I … yes, fully human." She was breathing too quickly. What had he sensed in her?

"Branch, Adeline," Viridi said, breaking through her worry, "would you please attend to Prince Werian and Princess Rhianne of the Agate Court?" He inclined his hand toward them as the wind shuffled the leaves high above the stairs and entranceway.

"What happens when it rains?" Nico looked up.

Viridi smiled and his beauty stole Isa's breath and drove her fears away. "We drink it in and enjoy the feel of the sweet water on our skin. What do humans do when it rains?"

Nico shrugged. "We tend to hide from it."

Viridi put a hand on Nico's shoulder. Nico flinched for a brief moment, then appeared to relax. Isa hated Ursane and the Brunes more than anything at that moment. They were the reason he was afraid to be touched. All those beatings...

She pressed her eyes together to fight her tears.

When she opened her eyes again, Viridi met her gaze, and she was surprised to see that he looked as though he understood at least the protective nature of what she was feeling. His lips pursed and he glanced down at Nico again. "Well, humans and dryad elves are different. Very different. But we are similar in that some of us are kind and others are not, but most are a combination of the two."

Nico frowned, not understanding.

She chewed her lip. "Sometimes I tell you stories and other times I'm really grouchy with you."

Face clearing, Nico nodded. "I see."

Julian offered his hand to Nico. Nico's eyes widened and he glanced to Isa. "It's fine," she said, hoping it really was.

"Let's give you a private room to wash and then you can eat."

"There's food?" Nico's voice was hushed with awe.

"Plenty." Julian gave Isa a nod before leading Nico to a room at the far end of the landing.

She worried about leaving him alone with the elf, but what choice did she really have? And honestly, if Nico didn't get some food and rest soon, he'd be in very bad shape. It was worth the risk.

With Werian and Rhianne heading off with the very tall Branch and the willowy Adeline, Isa allowed Viridi and Calva to take her into the nearest room.

The ceiling went up and up until a blur of sun-touched green blended with glimpses of the blue sky. Several alcoves sat along the chamber's far wall—one set with couches made of what felt like flower petals, another filled with woven pillows and baskets of carefully tied scrolls, and another with one hammock large enough for two.

The walls were simply the inside of the astounding tree, although vines grew from circular windows set into the wood. Bright blooms in deep red and rich purple decorated the lengths of green, and the windows didn't seem to have been cut out but instead it looked as though the tree had bent this way and that to create the space for light to enter. Dryad magic? Perhaps.

In the center of the room, a labyrinth curled in a great circle, its lines made up of darker or lighter wood, the hues alternating like a chess board.

"One may walk the labyrinth to solve problems," Viridi said. "Have you tried such a thing?"

"No, but I've seen them at various sacred places in my home kingdom of Wylfenden."

"There is one in Khem as well."

"Oh yes? Where? We only stopped at port. I didn't get the chance to see much of anything beyond the docks."

Viridi's eyes narrowed like he was angry on her behalf. "On the northeast coast of Khem, where very few tend to travel. Or so I have heard. I have never left this island."

"Why do you and your people remain here, isolated like this?" Isa asked.

Calva walked to a smooth trunk table and poured out what looked like a light wine into two wooden mugs.

Viridi accepted one of the mugs. "We prefer the quiet. We must maintain a place where the trees are respected and used properly. When trees are in pain, when people cut them down without first blessing the tree and asking for its aid, we feel that hurt. We are joined spiritually with every tree near us physically." He ran a thorned fingertip—because she'd decided that was what they looked like, thorns—over the rim before taking a sip.

"Do trees choose to give up their lives sometimes?" Isa

mimicked the way he'd touched the rim and then took a drink. The wine was cool and slightly sweet. Very good.

Viridi smiled at her as if he liked the fact that she had copied his gesture on the mug. "I have seen it happen, yes. A long time ago, we had a queen and she desired to see the distant shores, so she asked the trees to give up their lives so she could have a boat made of their timber."

"No offense, but didn't she feel badly asking for that just to travel about? I mean, I long to travel the world as well, but wouldn't it be difficult if you feel the trees' pain?"

"They feel no pain if proper spells are cast and sacrifices are made. Our queen thought it best to bring back humans for breeding."

Isa didn't know what to say to that except, "The humans were given a choice?"

"Of course. It was not accomplished in one venture to Khem, but in numerous trips to outlying villages, places where the queen spelled the folk to keep our secrets and maintain privacy."

"Interesting." He surely didn't think she could be persuaded to have dryad elf children, did he? Her face flushed as she studied his handsome features and let her gaze wander down his lean, muscled body. Loving him certainly wouldn't be terrible, but the children part ... she wasn't quite ready for that. She had Nico to think of.

She downed the rest of the wine, then wished she hadn't because her head began to swim.

Beyond the labyrinth, a simple rectangular table sat below three of those amazing windows. Calva set out large, flat leaves like plates and arranged piles of red berries, a tangled vegetable of some sort, and what appeared to be potato mash.

Her dramatically pointed ears catching the window's light, Calva bowed, then left the room.

Viridi pulled out a wicker chair for Isa and she sat, her stomach rumbling loudly. She laughed and he echoed the sound. Skies, she was glad she hadn't angered him. She didn't have the energy to try to constantly please someone even if it might mean her life.

"Enjoy," he said as he began to eat with his fingers.

"Forgive my bluntness, but may I ask some questions?"

"Of course. Nothing you say can offend me. You have no knowledge of our customs and you have already proven you do at least try to learn as you go, in what I am guessing is a sign of kind respect."

"Do you mean touching the rim of the wooden mug before drinking?"

"I do."

He snapped a berry between his sharp elven teeth. Mountain elves had teeth like that too, or so she'd heard. It made many humans like her nervous, but Viridi had thus far been incredibly gracious and gentle. She would trust him unless he proved she shouldn't. She was well and done with being a hateful, distrustful sort like the Brunes and Ursane. She wanted to be their complete opposite as much as possible.

After eating the entire plate of food in a way that she was fairly sure was ridiculously rude because her hunger just wouldn't be controlled, she wiped her mouth like he had done, using yet another leaf, this one as soft as lamb's wool.

"What does the ritual mean?" she asked, doing so again on her mug before taking a swallow.

"The gesture is meant to thank the tree that gave itself up to serve you."

"The way you talk about trees … I don't know if I can ever feel all right about sailing in a wooden ship or walking in my wood-heeled boots."

Viridi put his warm hand over hers, and her skin tingled at the contact, making her heart beat faster. His strange fingertips brushed the side of her wrist, just a faint touch, and a fantastic trail of goosebumps ran up her forearm.

He lowered his gaze on her, his wavy black hair slipping over his smooth forehead. "They live to serve those who appreciate the gift. They are not like you or me, or any other living creature in any realm. Their sensibilities are quite different. Don't be sad or tentative about working with wood as long as you are deeply grateful."

Isa exhaled in relief at that information, but as he pulled away gently she found herself disappointed and wishing he'd left his dryad hand on hers. How interesting he was … how different…

A beam of sunlight slipped past his sharp cheekbones and made his skin show a subtle green.

"You're lovely," she blurted, her face heating.

A quick grin stretched his lips, his eyes dark as night but glittering as if stars shone in their depths. How was she ever going to fall for a human after this experience? She was ruined.

"Thank you, Lady of the Sun." He glanced toward the door. "Calva? Can you please help the lady bathe?"

Calva appeared, bowing low with a fold of thick cloth draped over her arm.

"Bathing sounds amazing," Isa said. "Thank you very much for all of this. For helping us."

"Of course," Viridi said, giving her a hand out of her chair. "I will return shortly to talk with you if you are willing."

"Definitely."

Viridi left, and Calva led her into a side room she hadn't noticed. A large wooden tub filled with steaming hot water sat in the very center, and there was a stool beside it.

"How did you manage hot water here? I didn't see anyone coming or going." She looked for another entrance to the room, but saw none.

"We use runes to heat the water." She pointed at the bottom of the tub, and sure enough, a set of runes were worked into the wood there. "Water magic isn't our strength, but the trees help us work small miracles." Calva helped her undress, then the woman took the salt-crusted clothing and threw it in a heap in the corner while Isa climbed into the tub.

"Ah." It was exactly as glorious as she knew it would be. "It's been years since I've had a hot bath. Oh, don't look too affronted." She smiled. "I did manage very cold baths when I could in Khem and on the Brunes' ship."

Calva used a tiny bucket to draw up water. She poured it carefully over Isa's hair, then began to work in a sweet-smelling soap. "If you'd like, you can tell me what you went through. We night dryads are quite happy to listen."

"What are night dryads?"

"Most dryad elves must sleep during the day to gain energy from their home trees, trees with which they have a close relationship, built over time." She rinsed Isa's hair and squeezed out the excess water. "My kind rest at night in the moonbloom trees by the river. We are a rare type and we gain our strength from the sun's reflection off the moon. We are born with different magicks and different ways. Most of us choose to serve the royal family. It is tradition, and they offer us feasts and great rewards. My family has been serving the royals for over a thousand years, so the scrolls say."

"Fascinating. They are lucky to have you."

Calva smiled widely and began scrubbing Isa's back with a woven circle of what seemed to be linen.

"What does the prince's name mean? Thorned One? Is it because of his hands and ears? I noticed he doesn't look exactly like most of the dryad elves."

"Yes, but he also has great power. It hasn't yet bloomed in him, but we all know it will. He will be a mighty dryad and the protector of this island for centuries to come. We have waited ages for a powerful one like him to keep intruders away."

"Intruders like me?"

"No, you and your party are well-mannered. But in the

past, we have seen greedy humans and felt their fires and axes."

"I'm sorry for that."

"You didn't do it."

"But I'm human."

"Yes, but you are not responsible for your kind as a whole."

"I still feel bad that humans can be so terrible."

Calva murmured agreement and rinsed Isa with another tiny bucket of the steaming water.

"What powers will the prince have?"

"I think you should ask him. I don't want to speak behind his back."

"Oh, right. Of course. I will. Thank you for this bath, Calva."

With gentle movements, Calva helped Isa dry off with the thick fabric she'd brought, and then dressed her in a light green dress with a woven belt that hung at her hips. The material was wildly soft and Isa couldn't stop brushing her fingers down her sleeve and marveling at the turn of events—from servant with little hope of a future to a woman being treated like royalty on a legendary island of magic.

"You should sleep for a while. I can sense your body's fatigue." Calva pointed to the wide hammock in the far nook.

"Thank you. For all of this."

Calva gave her a smile before drawing the thick vines across the main doorway and leaving quietly.

The hammock could have been made of solid rock and Isa would have still fallen asleep immediately. But it was as soft as her dress, and she rested better than she had since childhood. Birdsong followed her into dreams of dark eyes, a deep voice, and the feel of a kind touch on the back of her hand.

Viridi peeked into the room where Julian had taken Isa's ward. Conversation bounced from the bathing room.

"And you're not going to make us leave? I want to stay here forever. Would that be all right or is that not? Do I need to ask for your king's permission? It seems like the prince likes us so maybe he'd say yes. What do you think? I'm very hungry. Do you think I could have a second meal right after the bath? I wouldn't eat much. Just maybe a little more of that red stuff? It was really delicious. I have never had that before. Do you like the red stuff?"

"Please, Master Nico, sit still for even one moment so I don't get this soap into your sensitive human eyes."

A chuckle left Viridi, and he pinched his lips to keep from laughing louder. Julian would be mortified if he knew Viridi had heard the trouble he was experiencing with one small youngling. He patted the doorframe, silently thanking the oak that made up his home, then left to find Felix.

Surely, Isa and the rest of them would sleep for a while. Prince Werian had sent Branch to Viridi requesting that word be given to the prince's crew out on his ship, just off the coast. Branch had appeared rather excited to have the chance to row over to the ship in the rarely used boat they kept hidden in the cave where the sea folk had once lived.

Viridi envied Branch. Viridi used to climb down to that cave when the tide was out and dig up runed seashells and other sea folk artifacts. He assumed there were sea folk still somewhere in the great expanse of oceans, but they hadn't seen any, and the scrolls never spoke of them beyond a scant mention in times of the distant past, in the age of the gods and goddesses, Arcturus of Air, Vahly of Earth, Nix of Fire, and Lilia of Water.

Leaving the oaken castle's side door, Viridi took the winding path through the kitchen garden. Brazenberries glistened, bright and ripe, on the bushes beside a stand of scorchpeppers—one of his favorite spicy treats. Basil and mint waved in the breeze as he walked by, their scent mingling in the air. Beyond the garden, the path wound into the deeper woods where Felix's home tree stood near a babbling stream.

Felix was going to hate being awoken, but it couldn't be helped. Viridi had to be sure someone he truly trusted knew about Isa and the others and his wishes for their good treatment just in case Viridi lost himself to the forest at large.

It had happened once already. In the middle of star basking, the jeweltrees' voices had grown loud in his head and he'd lost his ability to reason. He had regained his senses far from the place where he'd been enjoying the stars with the others. He had no idea what he had done in that lost time. And if the tales were true, being the Thorned One meant growing into a monster capable of great violence. It wasn't as if he were simply dreaming and meandering about the island as the wild trees influenced him. No, danger pounded through his blood. And he didn't want Isa and her party to suffer at the hands of his ridiculous father if he had to escape to the far side of the island, out of his mind.

Felix's tall pine tree bent its limbs to greet Viridi, who set a hand against the rough bark.

"Felix, I hate to bother you, but this is important. Wake, my friend." Magic shivered under Viridi's skin, his power reacting to his will and the position he held above Felix in the hierarchy of dryad elves. The sensation buzzed into his hand on the pine, and the wood beneath his palm warmed suddenly.

Viridi stepped back as the pine's trunk hazed with magic, emerald sparks blinking in and out as Felix appeared, eyes closed and face relaxed in rest.

Then Felix's eyes flew open and he swore, shaking his head. "You sapling's root, what in the name of every god are you doing? You know the night I had with Juno."

Viridi grinned and leaned against a nearby beech. "So

she was swayed by your keen knowledge of the female body?"

Felix rubbed his face viciously, then yawned, showing all his teeth. "I would love to say yes, but I think it was my interest in her study of the changing ocean temperatures."

Rolling his eyes skyward, Viridi laughed. "You two will marry in the library, won't you? Have your wedding night amongst the scrolls?"

Punching Viridi lightly in the stomach, Felix walked past him. "You might be the prince, but I'm not above being caged for thwapping you."

"Thwapping? Oh, do tell me what that will involve."

The sun hit Felix's face and he winced and stopped, whirling on Viridi. "Seriously, why did you wake me? It's not even sunset."

"A party of humans and one fae arrived."

"Armed?"

Viridi shook his head. "Why are we dryad elves so quick to think of their aggression? No, two were shipwrecked, and the other two arrived to be of help to them. One is Prince Werian of the Agate Court. He is in the company of his wife, Princess Rhianne."

"The one the redheaded Khem trader told us about?" Felix squinted into the forest canopy. His scar looked more pale than usual, his coloring wan because he hadn't rested long enough in his tree.

"Yes," Viridi answered, attempting patience with his scroll-loving friend.

"Is the Agate Court still a sub-kingdom of Lore?"

Another tolerant laugh left Viridi. "It is. Now, stop your mind from gallivanting into information no one but you and your beloved Juno care about and listen."

He told Felix all about Father and Isa's party.

Felix's big eyes studied Viridi's face. "You are deeply drawn to her. This is what you felt when you were distracted." He gripped Viridi's arm. "Eh, there's more you're not saying. She can't be your..."

"She is."

Mouth falling open, Felix stared. "She is your fated mate." His face stretched with a wide smile. "See? I told you that you shouldn't give up hope. This is wonderful!" He hugged Viridi roughly and Viridi clapped him on the back.

Breaking away, he thought about how to explain his trepidation. "I still don't know what is wrong with the jeweltrees. The poor woman is fated to mate with a man destined to become a monster. That's in addition to the fact that Father will fight this match with tooth and nail."

Felix blew out a breath. "Love is never easy."

"It's not easy for you and Juno?"

"For now, but it's so new."

Viridi nodded. He'd seen enough of mates to know there was almost always fighting even in the pairs that stayed together. Having a mate was a complicated situation full of passion and worry and knotted desires.

Felix spun dryad magic in his palm, the fresh green light sparkling brightly. He sometimes toyed with magic when he was in deep thought. "What are you going to do? Will you tell her everything?"

"I don't think it would do her any good." Viridi ran a thorned fingertip gently down a pine branch, encouraging the tree to grow with a swirl of warm magic. "I'm not sure what to do. Not yet. I'll take care of her as best I can for now and decide as things progress. I hate that she is in danger because of me."

"It's fate," Felix said. "She might surprise you with her strength. Not everyone is fated for the Thorned One."

Viridi wished he wouldn't say the title like that. "I set a waking dream on her."

"You what?"

"On both of us, actually. Quite accidentally," Viridi said. Waking dreams could lure the recipient and turn them into obsessed lovers. It was an old art and very dangerous. Viridi wished they weren't a skill his folk had.

"How did it feel?" Felix asked.

Viridi ran a hand over the back of his neck as the memories heated his blood. "Too real. Not like a dream, but like truth. Her body pressed against mine. Her breath was warm. It was terrible."

Felix laughed. "Terrible? Sounds rather lovely to me."

"You know what the waking dream can do."

"I do." At least Felix seemed abashed at being excited for such a dangerous happening.

Viridi straightened and took a deep breath. "As soon as she has rested from her ordeal, I'll apologize."

"I bet she didn't mind it too much. You're a good elven man. Anyone would be lucky to have your attentions."

"Thank you, my friend, but that is only true right now

while I have my mind firmly in my control, and well you know it. Can you promise to do your best to protect her from Father if I must leave, if the trees take hold of my senses? Or if I manage to persuade Father and the rest of you to leave for the Pearl Isles?"

Felix set his hands on Viridi's shoulders. "If she is still with us then, I will protect her like I protect Juno. But you're not going to lose your mind to the jeweltrees. You'll control this magic set on your soul. I have no doubt."

Hot tears burned Viridi's eyes, but he held them back. He tried to summon the words to thank him, but nothing he could say would have enough strength, so he simply set his hands on Felix's and nodded gravely as emotion attempted to sweep him away.

He bid Felix good rest and his friend stepped backward toward his home tree. The tree's magic shimmered and sparked, enveloping Felix until he was no longer visible.

For the first time in as long as Viridi could remember, he didn't wish to fall into a tree to sleep. He looked toward his oaken castle and smiled, Isa's face once more flashing through his thoughts. It was wonderful to be excited about life again, if only for a while.

As he strode down the path with the trees shifting slightly, nodding leaf-heavy limbs and rolling their roots to honor him, he tried to come up with a timeline.

When did he need to help Isa leave his island? How long would it be safe for her and Nico to be in his presence? He couldn't let them stay for such a time as to give up a life elsewhere. Even if he could hold off his transformation for moons, it would be wrong to persuade them to remain.

Just a few days, then.

He sighed, but picked up his pace, determined to make the most of the short visit with this woman whose warm soul called to him so strongly.

Claim her...

Drain her...

She can be yours...

The jeweltrees' voices threaded through his mind, brightening the image of Isa he'd conjured up and making his heart beat faster.

He whirled and faced the deepest part of the woods. "Stop."

The trees went silent.

Swallowing and shaking off a chill, he continued on to the castle.

Maybe just two days. Two days and then he would see them on their boat and gone safely. Two days and then he would somehow persuade all the other dryads to leave this island. He would give into the will of the forest and become the monster he was born to be.

CHAPTER 14
ISA

Isa woke to Calva holding a tray of steaming white buns. The dryad woman set them on the table where the afternoon sun glowed over the deep wood grain.

Isa climbed out of the hammock and sat at the table. "I think maybe I died and this is the blessed afterlife." The buns smelled sweet, and when she took a bite they were pleasantly chewy. "What's in these?"

"They are made from beans."

Reaching for a second, Isa paused. The light from the window glittered over the side of her hand. She stared, her blood going cold as she splayed her fingers. Tiny patches of the palest blue ran down her pinkie finger all the way to her wrist. The strange patches reflected the sunlight like pieces of window glass.

"What is it, my lady? Are you injured?"

Inhaling quickly and tugging her sleeve down, she forced a grin. "Oh, no. I'm fine. Sorry, you were saying?"

"The buns are made from beans."

"Interesting," Isa said, sounding a bit too loud. "They're my new favorite food." Perhaps she could ask Werian and Rhianne about her hand. Maybe Werian could heal her.

Calva smiled, nodding, and filled a wooden mug with wine. "I'll leave you to your meal, Lady of the Sun. The prince asks if he may visit you again."

Her heart jumped, and she turned in her chair, wishing to see him, but he wasn't there. "Yes, he's welcome anytime."

A small laugh bubbled from Calva and she bowed before leaving.

Isa drank down three big swallows of wine. Goddess save her, she was acting like a fool, leaping at any mention of Viridi. Calva would tell the prince how excited she was to see him and he would be put off by her ridiculous desperation.

It's not as if the prince truly cared for her. He should have—Isa knew her own self-worth; she was an intelligent woman with courage and a strong sense of loyalty. But he was a prince. He wouldn't see her unroyal self as someone to truly court.

Most likely he saw her as a pleasant distraction. Maybe even a plaything? No, she knew his heart. The moment on the coastline—when she'd first seen him—had somehow opened his very soul to her. But how could that be? It was impossible. She tapped the table and chewed her lip. She must have hit her head during the storm and her efforts to save Nico. That was the only answer that made sense.

Flattening her palms on the table, she breathed in slowly. All right. She would come at this with her head on straight. He simply needed to be made aware of her boundaries here and she had to find out what his expectations were.

"How was your rest?" Viridi's decadent voice flowed into the room.

"Wonderful. Thank you so much for your hospitality." She kept her gaze on the table and ignored her sweating palms. "I want to make certain we're clear here though." Facing him, she was hit once more with his otherworldly beauty. It didn't seem fair that a man so lovely could also be so kind, caring for Nico and her like he was. How was she supposed to withstand him and think reasonably before acting? "I am not going to deny there is a spark between us. Wait. Do you hate that word because, well, fire and trees…"

His grin released butterflies in her stomach. "I know what you mean. We are—"

She held up a hand—*not* the one with the odd patches of pale blue. "I simply want to allow Nico time to recover and perhaps get to know you more if you are interested in…in that. In me." She sighed at herself. She truly had the tongue of a poet. "I am incredibly flattered by your attention, but I don't want to be as reckless with my life as I've been in the past. I need time to think clearly."

He bowed low and remained there, looking up at her through his thick eyelashes. "I understand and respect your wishes, Lady of the Sun. I would never presume to be anything to you besides your polite host." The corner of his mouth lifted and his eyes went dreamy. "Unless of course, you request a deeper relationship."

Pleasant shivers spread down Isa's skin, and despite herself she was breathing too quickly, taking quick gasps that completely gave her away. She swallowed and looked away.

"Th-thank you."

"*Bien sûr*, Lady of the Sun," he said, using a dash of her native tongue and showing off his language skills. She was duly impressed. As isolated as they were here, it would have been easy for them to ignore the world, but his knowledge of distant tongues and customs showed he valued folk beyond his own shores.

"Why do you call me that?" *And please always call me that in that voice*, she thought, setting her goblet of wine aside. That stuff wasn't helping her avoid reckless behavior in the presence of this gorgeous creature.

"When I saw you, your soul warmed me."

She blinked. Had he had that strange, wonderful vision like she had? Had it been real and not the result of being knocked about in the sea? Had he felt their bodies pressing close, and imagined that kiss too? Surely not. "You seem to ... care for me ... and you don't know me at all."

"Dryad elves don't simply see a person. We can sense elements of your soul and heart, of who you really are."

"And you liked what you sensed of me?" She felt silly saying it, but her tongue didn't want to stop working and she found she was eager to know. It wouldn't be the first time or the last that her curiosity pushed her from dignified into foolish.

"I did. You remember when I first sensed you. On the beach." He looked away for a moment and pushed his hair away from his face. "I am sorry for that."

Warmth curled down her torso to gather low in her belly. *So he did experience it.* "What happened exactly? I thought I'd just been hallucinating due to the wreck and all of that."

"Dryad elves are born with the ability to draw in humans and fae—any creature, really. It's how we used to gain some of our energy, by draining it from others' bodies." He shuddered, echoing her own sentiments. "We gave up that brutal practice a century ago. My father told me the story. But the ability remains, and it is at times difficult to restrain, especially when we are strongly drawn to a soul." He met her gaze and invisible arrows pierced her heart. "Now, will you tell me of your life and how you came to be shipwrecked here?"

"I was adopted into a family of weavers and merchants. I ran the tapestry workshop I inherited from my parents. Tallying coins, keeping the books, working alongside the weavers most days. We lived in Nid de Lapin, a middling town on the edge of Wylfenden. I was never very happy, though I should have been. I didn't realize how wonderful my life was then. My tongue craved new flavors and my feet ached to walk new roads. Honestly, I felt trapped. But when a storm destroyed the workshop and our home, I lost everything and everyone. I was thrown into a darkness. I …

didn't know such things could happen to me, even though I'd seen tragedy hit many others."

A memory of her cousin, Louie, flashed through her mind—his wide-cheeked face marred with bruises from the storm's flying debris and his body lying lifeless on the cobblestones. She could almost smell the memory, the scent of the storm like deep ocean water. Her throat burned and she looked to Viridi to forget, to move past it.

Viridi's face reflected a layer of her grief, his sympathy evident in the set of his shoulders and the wrinkle between his eyebrows. "We see ourselves as untouchable when we are young, don't we?"

"I think so. Unless one is dealt a terrible hand from the start."

Viridi nodded and took a drink. She breathed in slowly, waiting for the pain of long ago to hide where it usually did, in the far corner of her mind.

"What did you wish to see when you dreamed of wandering?" he asked.

"The peaked mountains of the Balaur elves. My parents adopted me from merchants who had found me in the borderlands, left along the roadside. I have always wanted to see the dragons who live near there." She fisted the hand with the strange patches of faint color.

"Tracking wild dragons would be a dangerous hobby." He smiled like he thought it might be fun.

"Yes, but I've always...I don't know...I have dreamed of dragons since I was a child. I feel like they are misunderstood. I'd love to see them. And I want to visit the sacred forest of Illumahrah in Lore too. And of course, the spice markets of Khem, which I did get to see, albeit from a distance."

His lips pursed tightly and his eyes pinched for a moment, then he smoothed his face as if he had remembered something he didn't care to recall. Then he stood, pushing away from the table with the grace that princes always possess in stories and legends. He held out a hand.

"Will you dance with me, Lady of the Sun?"

"Now?"

He shrugged. "Now is all anyone has."

She couldn't help but smile like she'd received the best present in the world. "Of course."

He took her into his arms, settling his large hands at her waist. She lowered her hand—she'd been expecting him to lift one in the Wylfenden style—and placed it on his shoulder and did the same with her left hand as well, doing her best to keep her dress sleeve over the strangely textured and faintly colored patches along her pinkie and wrist.

He swayed and hummed a tune, the apple in his long throat bobbing slightly. Her fingers ached to touch the skin there and to lean closer, to take in his scent more deeply. It was as if the very forest itself had come to life and decided to embrace her as a lover.

Her knees grew weak and her head light, but his hold on her was firm, secure. She felt safer than she had in ages.

He began to sing, and Isa thought she might die right there from happiness.

"And to the shadows, I go,
To rest, to dream, to know.
And to the ocean, I go,
To see, to hear, to know.
And to the stars, I go,
To feel, to breathe, to know."

His chest rumbled as he sang the song again, his accent clipping the syllables in ways that made her want to listen to him forever. His hand slid farther down her back and urged her closer, and though it probably wasn't the wisest idea to cozy up like this to a stranger, she allowed it, enjoyed it. She'd never had the pleasure of a man's company like this. When her parents had died so suddenly, she'd been driven into early adulthood. Then the storm had happened and she'd lost it all, driven into indenture. Ever since, she'd been focused on Nico and keeping him alive. She hadn't had someone take care of her in years. So she let herself be held tightly by this gorgeous dryad prince and breathed in the scent of him and danced and danced as he sang song after song, lyrics that wove the story of his life here.

"Isa!" Nico rushed into the room, damp hair flopping around his ears and his feet clean and bare. He crashed into them, and Isa wrapped him in a hug. "Isn't this place wonderful? Julian brought me to the castle's courtyard where they have an enormous swing." He laughed. "I think I made him nervous with how high I went."

A bubbly feeling rose inside her heart and she regarded him, holding him at arm's distance. His bruises were gone, his little leg healthy and smooth beneath the short trousers

Julian had dressed him in. "You look very fine in your dryad elf clothing. Like a prince yourself."

"Indeed he does," Viridi said.

A knock sounded at the doorway and Isa turned to see Werian and Rhianne. Viridi waved them in, so they bowed their heads and entered.

Werian clasped his hands, then rubbed them together, that twinkle he always had in his eyes sparkling. "I think it's high time for a raucous feast, don't you think, Prince Viridi?"

Isa linked her arm in Nico's and they spun around and around, laughing up at the stars. To the Underworld with everything else. She just wanted to forget about the odd patches on her finger and wrist, the horrors they had been through, the worry about what had happened on the beach when she'd first seen Viridi. Tonight would be fun and nothing else. Nico deserved it. She deserved it. Later, after they'd lived a little, danced a lot, and eaten more, they would figure everything out.

The leaf-green glow of the dryad fires made her feel like she was inside the very heart of the woods. The magical fire had a lovely scent to it, akin to mint and lavender.

Grinning mischievously, Nico broke away and ran toward four dryad elves who were approaching with trays of food. They set the trays on the ground among the fires. Wooden bowls held walnuts, pistachios, light orange berries, and figs. One of the trays held cups and pitchers.

An elf poured out the drinks and Isa took an offered cup. She sipped it and tasted cloves, sage, and pomegranates.

"This is delicious," she said more to herself than anyone.

Nico was busy stuffing his face with berries.

"Are you enjoying yourself?" a deep voice said behind her.

Her heart stuttered and she turned to see Viridi. With the stars behind him and the dryad firelight illuminating his features, he looked like a god. His tousled dark hair fell over one eye and his lips quirked into a grin.

"Very much. Want to dance with me?" She wiggled her hips.

He laughed. "I would love to."

Taking his hand in hers and savoring the sparking heat that flooded her fingers, she pulled him toward the dancing. He circled her waist with one arm, pulling her close.

"I don't know any Wylfenden dances. Will you teach me?" he asked.

"But I quite like this particular dance," she said. *Why do I feel this way toward a stranger?* This was more than physical attraction. She was linked to him, her soul reaching for his. As much as she knew it was pure madness, she felt a true bond with him.

His body brushed hers and her insides melted in pleasure.

She smiled against his chest. "This is fantastic. If I'm asleep, don't wake me."

A chuckle rumbled through his chest, the vibration tickling her palm.

He bent closer to her and whispered a phrase in his language. A thrill sped through her blood even though she had no idea what he had said. His breath was sweet like the drink they'd been serving. He kissed her neck softly and she practically purred.

Pulling away, he studied her face. "Am I frightening you?"

"No." She tugged his tunic and brought him close again. "That was a good shiver, Prince Viridi. A very good shiver."

A gleam of pride shone in his deep, dark eyes and he kissed her ear. "Such funny little ears you have, lovely girl."

"You're the one with the funny ears, my lord," she said, her words coming out breathy. Her heart was going to thrust itself through her ribs if he kept this up. But at least she'd die happy.

An elven man with a scar across the side of his mouth approached them, smiling.

Viridi moved away from her a step. "Felix," he said, clapping the dryad elf on the back. "Isa, meet my dearest friend, Felix."

Felix bowed to Isa, then took her hand and squeezed it softly before releasing her. He wore a necklace of acorn caps and dark sweet gum leaves. "I am delighted to see you. Viridi has spoken very highly of you."

His words were warming, but... "He knows so little about me. What did he say?" She grinned and raised eyebrows at Viridi.

Viridi smiled and let Felix continue.

"He claimed your soul was the brightest he'd seen in his life and that the love you hold for your ward speaks to your big heart."

She opened her mouth to speak, but nothing came out.

Viridi's grin fell away and his gaze turned serious. "It's true." He glanced at Felix as if to ask him for advice and Felix shrugged. Viridi looked at her again. "Have you heard of fated mates?"

Isa's heart stumbled and rolled over a rib. "Like they have in Lore?"

"Yes," Felix said, his gaze asking Viridi if it was all right for him to be there, "but a dryad elf's fated mate is slightly different."

"You know more than I do," Viridi said to Felix. "Tell us what you've learned in your beloved scrolls."

Felix made a face at Viridi and it was obvious these two had grown up together, teasing one another like brothers. Felix turned to Isa. "When a dryad elf sees their fated mate, they immediately feel the bond and their mate does as well."

Isa rubbed her sweating palms on her dress. Fated mate. That was what had happened on the beach when she'd seen him in the tree line, when they'd been together in mind and soul and spirit, why he felt so familiar.

Viridi's black eyelashes lay on his high, sharp cheekbone, the flesh there shimmering subtly in the green firelight. Was he afraid to look at her, to see a possible rejection?

Her heart shuddered and cracked wide open for him.

She took his hands, not caring if he saw the strange markings on her pinkie and wrist. This was too important to shy away from. His eyes flew open and Felix stepped away, giving them a modicum of privacy.

"Do you accept the bond?" Viridi said. "There is much I must tell you. It's not happy news. Don't say yes until you hear everything."

She held his hands tightly and leaned closer. His scent flooded her and she breathed him in. "I don't care what you're about to say. I can't deny this...this link between us. I've been questioning it, of course, but I know you, Viridi."

He inhaled sharply, his chest moving.

"Whatever the challenges, I choose you." She lifted her chin.

His lips parted and he bent his head.

"My prince," an elf said, eyes wide and obviously uncomfortable with interrupting.

"Yes?" Viridi's gaze stayed on Isa's face.

She was completely lost for him.

The wide-eyed elf cleared his throat. "The young dryads from the northern shore are here to offer fealty to you and the king."

"Ah, of course." Viridi looked at Isa. "Would you greet them as my consort?"

"What exactly does consort mean?"

Chuckling, he held out his arm. "It means I am courting you."

She raised an eyebrow and attempted to appear reluctantly

agreeable even though pleasure stirred in her blood. He didn't need to grow overconfident about her foolishly powerful and sudden feelings for him. She wanted to at least pretend she had some control over the situation. "All right."

They walked past clusters of elves drinking and playing dice games on smooth tree stumps. A knot of elves laughed around a taller elf who spoke with a lilting voice and whose hands moved around dramatically. Perhaps he was telling a story. Other elves danced, the womenfolk's gazes flicking to Viridi like they couldn't help themselves.

Isa understood the feeling, and couldn't help but grin at the fact that she was the one walking with him.

Another group of elves spoke with Werian and Rhianne about life at the fae court and beyond.

"You should have seen his wyvern," Rhianne was saying. "His name was Ivar and he was the size of a hawk. But he was a very good fighter..."

Viridi led her to a set of tree-formed thrones. There was one for his father, the king, and one for Viridi. Viridi extended a hand toward the empty throne.

"Please sit, my lady."

"But what about you?"

The king's gaze burned into her cheek. She could guess he was evaluating this new relationship with a heaping dose of caution.

With a smile, Viridi turned away from her and set his thorned fingers on the maple beside the thrones. He whispered something that sounded melodic and ancient.

Grass-green light flickered around his hand and arm, and the tree began to creak.

A fluttering went through her stomach as the maple bent slightly, like a very large man bowing. A new branch grew from the tree's middle and reached outward, before lengthening to touch the ground. The branch widened and glimmered with green light until it was a near match to the other two thrones.

"Neat trick," she said, grinning.

Viridi inclined his head and seemed to be waiting for her to sit. She did so and he settled himself beside her, his arms alighting on the maple arms of the dryad throne.

She almost laughed at the absurdity of the situation. Not two days ago she'd been a servant well on her way to being a slave. Now, she sat on a throne with the legendary dryad elves. Maybe this was a grand hallucination and soon she'd wake up on the Brunes' ship. Stars and goddesses, she hoped not.

The line of dryad elves before the thrones looked at the king and the prince expectantly and a hush traveled through the feasting area. Even the fires burned lower in their stone circles as if the magic that made them knew the import of this moment.

The elves began speaking in their tongue, quick and soothing. It was a lovely language even if she didn't understand a word.

A male elf with a vest made of what looked like large acorn caps knelt and held out his hands palms up. The king stood, approached him, then set his own palms on the supplicant's. Dryad magic shimmered between the point of contact. Viridi's father returned to his throne and Viridi stood, doing exactly what the king had done. Then when the glimmer of green magic faded, Viridi gestured to Isa.

Did he expect her to know what to do? She chewed her lip and stood. "I'm Isa Bisette. *Enchanté.*" She hoped mixing the common tongue with her own Wylfenden language wouldn't be too confusing.

The elf's eyes widened briefly, but he bowed to her. "My light is your light, Desired of My Prince."

Desired of My Prince? Was that...? She swallowed. Was that what he'd asked them to call her? The vision she'd shared with Viridi on the beach before they'd met flashed through her memory and sent heat rushing to her cheeks.

"Thank you," she said. She had no idea what else to say.

Rhianne nodded to her across the crowd. Werian leaned on a tree and watched, his gaze wary and his purple-black hair catching the light.

A woman came forward and bowed swiftly. Her blonde hair brushed the leaves on the ground, and the points of her ears showed above a small braid that circled her head. When she straightened, her amethyst glare pinned Isa down.

"Desired of My Prince," she said, using the strange title, "I am Helena of the eastern tribes. I confess I am surprised you are a human."

Viridi stepped in front of the elven woman and flexed his thorned fingers. There was a sound like far-off thunder as forks of bright green light flickered around his body. He loomed over her and she bowed low, her gaze on the earth.

"Speak to my lady again in such a manner," he said, "and you will find yourself without a tribe."

Hushed murmurs spread through the crowd, and Rhianne and Werian traded a whisper.

The dryad elves would hate her if she didn't fix the situation. Viridi's protectiveness was warming, but this was a bit much.

"I understand that it's a shock," she said. "Believe me, I'm as amazed as you are."

The woman—Helena—peered at Isa with that steely purple gaze of hers, but she didn't fully lift her head or come out of the bow. Considering Viridi was still standing over her like he was about to rip her head off, Isa didn't blame the woman. She started to say something to Viridi, but the woman spoke first.

"I reject your desire," Helena said.

CHAPTER 16

ISA

Isa held her breath as Viridi visibly tensed.

The ground trembled, and the trees all around shook like a storm was approaching. Viridi's hands splayed at his sides. He stepped sideways and turned, throwing his head back, the veins in his neck and along his forearms standing out. With a snapping and cracking sound, his crown of branches grew until the tips of it brushed the lower limbs of the maple and the pines.

"Viridi!" Isa called out over the rumbling of the earth.

"Leave him," the king said, his voice barely audible. He was grinning like a madman. *How can he be pleased with whatever this is?* It was horrifying.

"Go," Viridi said to Helena, his voice echoing magically through the trees. "You are banished, Helena."

The woman spun and ran into the forest. The others didn't watch her flee. All eyes were on Viridi.

Then Viridi looked at Isa.

She went cold from head to toe.

His dark irises had gone white as moons. Black leaves grew from the ends of his eyelashes, and with a sound like a slithering snake, those same black leaves sprouted along his collarbone and across his wrists. His thorned fingers elongated. His lips pulled away from his suddenly very sharp teeth.

Isa ran to Nico and put him behind her. *What is happening?* "Help him!" she shouted to the wide-eyed elves. "Viridi!"

The scent of moss and green wood rose in the air as Viridi stalked toward her, his head tipped downward and his teeth still showing.

Swallowing, she spread her shaking arms wide. "Viridi, please. I know you're in there." By some magic, she already knew his heart and soul. But none of his goodness showed in his milk-white eyes.

His lip curled and his tongue undulated between his sharp teeth. A sound between a staccato purr and a growl came from his mouth.

Sweat trickled down her neck and the tiny hairs on her arms rose.

The king stood slowly as if he too were afraid of spooking his son. "He is the Thorned One, and this is his true form."

The other dryad elves stepped back, shoulders hunching, watching with unblinking eyes. A mother with a crown of braids gathered her three barefooted children behind her.

Felix ran to get between Isa and Viridi, his hands spread wide. "Prince, you aren't yourself. You don't want to do this. We don't drain humans. We haven't for ages."

Drain?

Rhianne whipped out her wand and aimed it.

"Wait!" Isa motioned for them to move back. "Let me talk to him. Viridi, it's me. Isa. Remember?"

The king moved his arm and emerald stars flew from his fingertips. The roots under Rhianne broke from the ground, ripped her wand away, and tossed the magical weapon into the forest. Werian grabbed Rhianne and pulled her away from the undulating roots.

Scowling, the king continued as if Isa and Felix were nothing and their words had no meaning. "We welcome his transformation. Everything the Thorned One does is for us, the dryad elves. He is our promised savior, our leader in these changing times. He will bring us back to our former glory." Raising his arms, he eyed the crowd. "Bow to him."

And they did.

The king faced Isa as Viridi walked slowly toward her. "And embrace your fate, human woman."

"My fate?" Isa's voice trembled as much as her body.

"Embrace your fate as the honored sacrifice to our ancient forest."

Isa pushed Nico toward Rhianne and Werian, then she looked to the king, trying not to run screaming from Viridi.

"I'm not embracing anything, Your Highness. Viridi, I'm going to take Nico and go back to your lovely home to wait for you. We will find a solution to this."

Viridi blinked repeatedly, and tipped his head to one side, like he was fighting this monstrous side of himself. Then he reached out his branched hand. A chill shot through her chest. Pale blue wisps of light appeared over her heart, then flew shimmering to Viridi who inhaled them.

He was stealing her energy.

She'd read of magic like this when she was a child, of rare creatures who could siphon life from others and use it to grow more powerful.

"Viridi..." Her lips didn't want to work.

Vines laced Werian, Rhianne, Nico, Felix, and anyone else who ran at Isa to help.

What could she do to wake Viridi up? He wasn't a monster. His soul was as known to her as her own. She felt the tug of the bond between them, that tug that had drawn her mind to his on the beach.

Closing her eyes and gritting her teeth, she tried to ignore the terrible cold and focus on the bond, the link. She imagined it being a chain with links of silver and gold. Still only using her mind, she imagined the pale wisps leaving her winding around the chain. She yanked it hard.

The chill left her body immediately and she opened her eyes to see Viridi releasing all the others. He was trying to speak, but couldn't seem to get anything out.

"Go!" Werian snagged her arm and dragged her into the forest.

Rhianne and Nico were already waiting with two other dryad elves.

They started to run.

Branch, the tall servant from Viridi's tree castle, caught up with them. "I'm sorry your visit has come to this."

They hurried around a bend and under impossibly massive roots that had grown over the path. Her heart ached for Viridi. He hadn't meant to attack her. There was something wrong with him and his magic. The scent of sulfur and rot filled her nose...

Calva appeared from the shadows, her dark pink lips gone pale. She took the lead. "I know a shortcut to the beach. Come."

"The beach?" Isa slowed even as Nico pulled at her arm.

"Yes," Rhianne said. "You certainly don't mean to stay now. We can be on board our ship in an hour. We can take you anywhere you wish to go."

"I know it's complete madness, but I truly believe he didn't mean to lose his head back there. He needs our help. Did you see his father? We can't leave kind Viridi to this fate. His father will only encourage the beast inside him to rise up. He's like Seigneur Brune, power hungry. We have to help him, alongside his fellows, to find a way around this problem."

"This is who he is," Branch said, voice soft.

Needles pricked Isa's heart. "You don't have any hope for your prince at all?"

Branch shook his head. "I wish I did, but the legends speak of the Thorned One. We knew it was him, but we had hoped he'd avoid the full transformation."

"I, for one, never thought he would lose himself like that," Calva said. "But the legends appear to be true."

Branch nodded. "We hoped in secret because you are right that the king wishes to see Prince Viridi dominate this island, as well as any land they can reach by boat. But seeing him like he was just now ... there is no hope. You must escape while you have a chance. There is no one who can fight him when he is transformed. He is earth magic personified. Unbeatable."

"Except if someone has flint and a striker?" Werian raised his eyebrows. "It's true, is it not? If he is the lord of trees, he most likely burns like one."

The dryad elves scowled at Werian and refused to speak the rest of the way to the beach, but Isa didn't have any room in her mind for any of that. She could only think of Viridi's moon-white eyes and the way he'd tried to shake off his transformation when she'd spoken to him.

Was she really going to leave him like this?

He was being used by his father. That much was clear even if she knew next to nothing about this place or dryad elves. She'd seen enough of malevolent men to know one when she saw one, and the king was a prime example.

Nico tugged on Isa's dress. "I liked it here too, but we have to leave, don't we?" The whites of his eyes showed all the way around his irises. He walked so closely to her that it was difficult to stay upright.

"Of course," she said, giving in and trying to push her heart to the side and the bond to the back of her mind. Of course she would take Nico to safety. If it had just been her, she might have stayed to help Viridi, but she was Nico's only family and he needed her and a safe place to grow up. It would be atrocious for her to risk his life for the foolish desires of her heart. Viridi might not even want her help.

"Listen," Werian said to Branch and Calva, "I apologize for offending you, but your king did try to have our friend eaten by his very scary son. Can you really blame me?"

Branch and Calva exchanged a glance. "I suppose we can forgive you, fae prince, based on your loyalty to your friend."

He bowed and swept a hand dramatically across his body. "A thousand thank yous."

Rhianne curtseyed and gave them a sympathetic smile.

Isa followed them over the sand, the grains shifting under the shoes Viridi had given her. She faced the woods as Rhianne lifted her wand and sent out a blazing spark of purple light to hail the ship bobbing off the coast. The others talked, but Isa didn't join in. It was madness, but her heart was breaking.

Never before had a man captured her attention like Viridi. Not once had she experienced such powerful desire and care for a person before even getting to know them. She knew, without a doubt, she would never love anyone with the intensity that she would have loved Viridi if given the time here with him. He was special. A wonder. A complex and fascinating soul. Visions of him and memories of his words would echo through her dreams forever.

CHAPTER 17
VIRIDI

From the shadows of the jeweltrees, Viridi watched her go. Blood shushed in his ears and he dug his thorned fingertips into the trunk beside him, hand shaking. His nostrils flared, seeking her scent in vain. The tree winced—not as an elf would but as more of a dimming of its energy, a ripple of discomfort that echoed through Viridi's body. He detached his sharp hold on the tree, apologizing absently. How was he going to survive this? His soul shuddered as she moved farther and farther away.

He'd found himself after she'd fled, and between Felix and Father, he'd heard the story. Squeezing his eyes shut, he wished he could beg forgiveness for taking energy from her like that. He hadn't been aware of himself, but it was no excuse really. He'd known it was a risk and that the jeweltrees could taint his mind, and he'd still insisted on spending time with her.

Once Viridi had his own mind again, Father had

demanded that Viridi fetch back his sacrifice. He had staunchly refused.

"Do it," a voice said behind him.

He turned to see Felix loping from the deeper darkness of the forest. His eyes were bloodshot and Viridi knew he was the cause of his distress.

"Do what?" Viridi looked again toward the skiff. Isa, Nico, Prince Werian, and Princess Rhianne were boarding their ship. He could still feel the beat of Isa's heart next to his. It was an illusion, of course—he didn't hold any part of her inside his corporeal body. But the feeling made his head swim all the same.

"Go get her. Call her back," Felix said.

Felix's hand on his shoulder was warm and comforting, so he eased away from him. He deserved no comfort.

"I can't. It's too dangerous and you know it. Pretend for a moment you aren't my friend and instead you're hers. What would you say then?"

"I don't think fate would tease you both like that. The way you defended her... I know you, Viri. You'll find a way to solve this and she may be the key. Also, I'm so glad you banished Helena. She should have been sent on her way when she denied the sick ones a portion of her harvest last year. She's the real beast here."

Viridi pushed his emotions down, down, down. He had to focus on his plan. "What did Father say about the Pearl Isles?"

"He won't consider it," Felix said. "He shows only delight at what happened."

Viridi sighed and squinted as the distance swallowed Isa and the ship. He shivered. He wished he could leave the island, but he feared the jeweltrees here would blame the others for his absence and would refuse to feed them. *Or worse.* "I will have to motivate him."

"I don't like the sound of that."

"Because you're far more intelligent than my father." Father was foolish not to fear him.

Felix glanced at the tall oak beside them.

"Don't worry about the trees telling our secrets. I can hear them, and they don't care about any of my father's wishes."

Felix touched Viridi's shoulder again. "I'll never give up on you. You can't talk me out of that."

He hated how much he loved hearing that. "But you'll keep urging the council and my father to leave the island as I wish, right?"

"I will. What are you going to do to motivate them, to make them believe you are a threat not only to the outsiders but to us?" He pronounced the last two words with a tone that said he knew the act would be a horror. He was correct.

Felix glanced at the place where the skiff had been dragged ashore. Beside those marks in the sand, a broken barrel and a sea-washed cloak that must have belonged to the wrecked ship listed in the tide.

Viridi smiled sadly at Felix. "Go back to your tree. You need sleep. Your fatigue is tugging at me like an ocean current."

Felix patted Viridi's back once, nodded, and left, seemingly content to let Viridi keep his plan a secret.

Viridi let the wind filter through his hair and over the wooden tips of his ears and fingers. He imagined he could hear the ship cutting through the waves on its path to Khem or wherever else they might go. He pretended the sweet sound of a curious lady with a smile as warm as sunlight spoke of adventures to come, pretended the song of her voice cascaded through the wind. Isa was too far to truly hear now, but it was a pleasant fiction.

Turning, he resolved to rest in a tree until the others woke for starlight. Tomorrow afternoon, or maybe in the night, he would find a way to turn his father toward a future far away from here.

Felix disappeared into the shadows, and Viridi melded with the largest jeweltree on the shoreline. Pushing his longing for Isa away, he turned his mind to how he could strike terror into the hearts of his people.

Because if he failed, they were all as good as dead.

He knew when he rose fully as the Thorned One, he would end them all in his rage and thirst. He was no savior.

He was a nightmare coming to life.

CHAPTER 18
ISA

Isa tried to be happy. She was indeed incredibly grateful to Werian and Rhianne and the crew for healing and feeding them, and for the hammocks for proper seagoing sleep. But only two days had passed and already she longed to fling herself overboard and swim back to the dryad island and Viridi.

She wanted it so badly she could hardly keep herself on board. Moon-shaped cuts showed in the railing beneath her fingernails as she gripped the painted wood trim and tried not to be a madman.

The *Nucklavee's Daughter* was a beautiful ship with sleek black trim, touches of brass, and sails as white as summer clouds. Even the crew's sleeping quarters were tidy. Well, perhaps not tidy, but not horrible either. The decks were regularly swabbed with water Rhianne magicked to smell of lemons.

But still, Isa hated it because it wasn't Viridi's castle.

Goddess, I'm a whiner, a brat, an ungrateful lout. She shook her head and attempted to be a normal person.

Rhianne handed Isa a crockery mug of what smelled like rum and oranges. "You must tell me what's wrong, love." The swinging lanterns along the ship's side made her chestnut hair shimmer.

Isa took a sip; the rum burned its way down her throat. "I couldn't possibly. I'd lose any shred of respect I've gained from you."

Rhianne's smile had soft edges. "Not possible."

"Even if what I wish were happening is completely and utterly mad?" The crescent moon's glow touched Isa's fingers. She tucked her hand into her pocket to hide the strange skin on the edge of her palm and wrist. It was spreading.

"As a left-handed cobbler's niece," Rhianne said, "I traipsed into the forest of Illumahrah to meet the Matchweaver Witch of that time. I was convinced there was a match out there for me despite the warnings and mocking of my fellow villagers, as well as the wolves in the woods."

"So you're saying you're mad and thus you'll understand a likeminded woman?"

Rhianne laughed. "I'll drink to that." And she did.

Isa shook her head.

"No, truly," Rhianne said, "I am as practical as you seem to be and yet I plunged into the dark forest with no support, and went after what I wanted. Werian and I, we are dreamers. And dreamers often live a life no one else can even imagine."

"How can you be a dreamer and also practical?" Isa asked. "They're opposites."

Werian leapt down from the rigging, where he'd been easing a sail with a man named John who was as big as two Werians—and the fae prince was far from small. "It's all about balance. Dream impossible things. Don't hinder your heart. Then, take simple, practical steps to attain that dream."

The rum made Isa's head feel fuzzy. Suddenly the truth was pouring from her mouth. "I wish I could explore that dryad island and get to know the prince."

"Even though that plan might see you dead?" Werian smiled as he asked, which made Isa like him even more.

Rhianne winked.

They truly were mad. Perhaps she was as well.

"Yes," Isa answered.

"Turn us around, John," Werian called out to the incredibly tall first mate.

"Aye, aye, Captain." John began shouting orders in the cutting tone of his coastal Lore accent. "We're changing tack. Ready about!"

"Hard alee!" the crew called back.

Eamon turned the wheel, his lips pulled back and cheeks darkening with the effort as the ship's bow passed through the eye of the wind.

They were headed back to Viridi, back to danger. Isa's hand went to her wildly beating heart. She couldn't do this.

She shot to her feet, knocking over an empty crate behind her. "Wait!"

Werian frowned. "I thought this is what you wanted? We'll come with you if you like. I know a few crew members that would gladly say yes to a new adventure. Eamon for one doesn't have the good sense to say no, and never has a day in his life. Little Nico can remain on the ship where he'll be safe. I will post men to stay with him."

"What's happening?" Nico climbed out of the darkness from belowdecks.

"Wait. No. Just ... I can't do this," Isa waved her hands in an attempt to get the crew to stop changing course. "Stay the course to Khem and I'll find work there. It was only the rum talking."

"You're certain?" Rhianne asked. "I am happy to indulge in your madness." She grinned with all of her teeth and looked every bit the pirate and nothing like a cobbler.

"I'm sure. I don't want to risk..." Isa said, trailing off. Nico was staring up at the stars. The sight of him healthy and happy warmed her through and through. She leaned close to Rhianne. "I can't lose him to my ridiculously curious nature."

"You're assuming things would go badly," Werian said over Rhianne's shoulder.

Rhianne raised an eyebrow and looked at him. "Well, there was the part where Isa's handsome fellow turned into a tree monster who seemed inclined to murder."

He shrugged. "Your choice, Mademoiselle Isa." He spoke in the Wylfen tongue, surprising her.

She answered in her home's language. "When Nico wiggled his way into my life, my heart left my chest to live in his."

Werian smiled and Rhianne glanced to Nico, obviously picking up at least some of what they were talking about.

"I love him more than any adventure," Isa said in the Lore trade tongue so that Rhianne would be sure to understand.

Werian called for the men to reset the course to Khem.

"Of course you do," Rhianne said. "He is an adventure in himself." Rhianne grabbed Nico's arm and whirled him around as John pulled a shawm out of a container near the compass box and began to play.

"To Khem," Werian reminded the crew. "And while we go, there shall be dancing!"

CHAPTER 19
ISA

Attempting to push thoughts of Viridi's eyes to the back of her mind, Isa joined in the dancing and was soon laughing and showing the steps to an old Wylfen basket dance to several incredibly drunk sailors.

A sailor named Eamon tied his yellow beard into knots and sang a story about a creature from the distant land of Skyedon Ash.

It was an amazing night of revelry, and Isa was indeed incredibly grateful for her and Nico's change in fate. Even if she did incessantly think of Viridi, her heart pinching painfully as she imagined him struggling against whatever dark magic had hold of his soul...

She woke in her hammock, Nico snoring lightly in another to her left, and John snoring very loudly to her right.

A shout pierced the chorus of snores. "Dragon!"

Isa went cold all over.

Nico sat up. "What did they say?"

"Dragon."

And then they were all scrambling out of their hammocks and running up the stairs to the deck.

A shadow blocked out the morning sun. A strange, piercing whistle cut the hush of the waves on the ship.

Guided by Werian, John dashed across the deck behind them and began barking orders.

Nico gasped loudly.

Azure wings and a glittering body passed overhead.

A shiver of dread and a thrill of excitement shot through Isa as she ducked and grabbed a knife that was sitting beside a coil of rope. *A dragon!*

Then a ship drew up beside them, three people on the deck painfully familiar.

Isa's stomach turned forcefully and she stumbled, falling against the main mast.

She had to act quickly.

She snatched John's black cap from his head and shoved it into Nico's hands. "Nico, put this on."

John merely gave her a quick glance, and must have seen what she was about because he didn't argue. The cap swallowed Nico's mop of hair. Heart pounding, Isa looked for anything with which to disguise herself.

"Take this." Eamon handed her a kerchief and an eyepatch—the type they used to cover one eye so that when they went belowdecks they could uncover the other eye and see better in the dim.

She donned the kerchief and tried to tie it, but her hands were shaking too much.

"Allow me," Rhianne said, appearing from belowdecks with her wand in her belt. She finished the knot and helped Isa slide on the patch. "I don't know what's happening, but we have your back, Isa."

Isa wanted to hug her.

"Ahoy!" the horrible voice of Seigneur Brune carried over the water. "What is your business on this route? I don't recall seeing a paid passage for such a vessel when I docked in Khem."

Werian snorted a laugh. "You paid to sail this strait?"

Rhianne stood beside him, wand out. "He knows nothing, poor thing."

"That's no poor thing," Nico said, his voice a snarl. "Those are the Brunes."

"The ones who enslaved you?" Werian asked, his voice threaded with danger.

Leaning against the ship's side, Isa nodded and gripped the knife tightly. Her fingers ached to throw the blade and pray for miraculous justice. "I should have wished them dead while I had the chance."

Werian raised his eyebrows. "What does Seigneur Brune plan to do with that small dragon of his? Despite its youth, I'm properly frightened. They have fire from an early age, or so my friend, Prince Dorin, has told me." He faced Rhianne. "My little fox, I don't think we should disguise ourselves with glamour. It's possible we may need to use our titles to see this situation through."

"Agreed," Rhianne said.

"I don't think Seigneur Brune will outright attempt to take the ship or steal from you," Isa answered, "but he may encourage you to make a less-than-profitable trade with him ending up on the more pleasant side of things."

"That's just stealing creatively," Werian said. "What do you want, good sir?" he called out over the water as the dragon circled above. Werian's fae voice somehow carried powerfully across the noise of the waves and sails.

Dame Brune blew a whistle three times and the dragon flew lower, its tail brushing the edge of the mainsail. Several of the crew on the *Nucklavee's Daughter* whispered curses and prayers in turn.

"We were wondering if you'd ... *visited* any new islands out this way," Seigneur said through a conical speaking tube.

Ursane stood on his other side, her tall frame and the way she stood an echo of Isa's nightmares. Surely, she couldn't see this far in this harsh light...

Rhianne cut a look at Werian.

"No, good sir," Werian lied. "I didn't think there was a landing spot anywhere until one sailed to Skyedon Ash or west to Reyvik."

"Ah. Of course. My mistake," Seigneur said. "Travel safely." He turned to shout orders to the crew.

"How did he get a new ship so fast, Isa?" Nico blinked at her and she pushed him behind Rhianne just in case.

"When you have money," she said, "you can do a great deal that seems impossible. Hence the dragon."

Nico nodded. He was a little green. "Do you think they saw us?"

"No. The ships were too far apart," Isa answered, "and we had our disguises on. We're safe."

The dragon shrieked above them, sending chills down Isa's back. Her dreams of dragons hadn't been vivid enough. This dragon was glorious—the bright color, the coiling strength in its body... It was frightening, but also so very beautiful. She felt such a pull toward the creature, an empathy. She wished with her whole heart that the dragon wasn't with the horrible Brunes and was instead flying free in the mountains of Balaur, where she had been born.

A sharp sound pierced the air and the dragon turned sharply and flew toward the Brunes' new ship.

"She's using a whistle to control the dragon," Rhianne said.

"What did they do to that dragon to make it obey?" Feeling sick to her stomach, Isa watched the creature wheel toward them, then land on an upper deck that seemed designed for that purpose exactly.

"I don't want to know," Werian muttered. "But this changes things."

"What do you mean?" Isa handed the short crewman his patch and kerchief, thanking him.

John picked up Nico and pulled his cap lower on the boy's face to make him giggle.

"Those beasts are headed for the dryad island," Werian

said. He began giving quick orders to John, who then repeated and detailed them to the crew.

"But surely the wards that kept everyone from seeing it are back up?"

Isa remembered that the storm had broken the magic.

"I would think so," Rhianne said. "So what is going through your head, darling?" she asked Werian, who had returned to her side.

"Well, we can trail the Brunes and inform them that if they harm the dryad elves in any way, the full force of the Agate Court will strike them." His gaze flicked to Isa.

"Why would you do that?" Isa asked.

"Because you care for the lad," Werian said, his eyes going soft. Then he faced the direction of the island. "And people like the Brunes should be shown they can't sail about the world terrorizing and taking what they want."

"What's our plan?" Rhianne asked.

"I'll take down the dragon as gently as possible. I can heal the creature afterward if I manage to shoot him down over land. You, my love, use your witch fire on that woman with the whistle."

"Aim for her heart," Isa said, recalling Nico's bruises. She wasn't even a little bit sorry.

Nico nodded, his eyes narrowed.

Werian put a hand on Nico's shoulder like Nico was a fellow warrior and not a small boy. Nico stood straighter, pride shining in his bright blue eyes.

"Isa," Werian said, "you, John, and Eamon head for Viridi."

"I have no idea where he will be."

"I'm guessing your intuition will tell you," Werian said. "Do you agree, lady wife?"

Rhianne smiled. "My witch's instinct says you're fated for one another, or at least deeply connected in some way. And if you don't feel a tug in one direction or another, then go to his castle."

"All right." Isa looked at Nico. "I want you to stay aboard and stay safe."

"I will. Even though I want to fight for you. I'm your brother." His blue eyes flashed, daring anyone to deny it.

She blinked, her heart shaking. "Yes, you are," she confirmed, feeling the new truth of it. They might not be blood kin, but he was still her brother and she loved him so very, very much.

Nico hugged her fiercely as the ship rolled over a wave and the water crashed. The wind whipped his short hair as he pulled away. "Viridi won't hurt you, right?"

"I hope not. I don't think so." She didn't want to lie to him.

"Once we incapacitate the dragon, we will have this battle well in hand," Werian said. "Not to brag, but I'm fairly good with a bow. My wife here is better, and she is, of course, a witch."

Rhianne tapped the end of her sheathed dryad. "I will fight hard and get to you as quickly as possible, Isa. If things go badly, just return to the ship or find shelter along the beach. We will find you. Fae can scent people very easily."

"We are hard to kill too. It will be easy," Werian said.

"Dragonfire kills everything," Nico said.

"True." Werian patted him on the back. "I don't plan to get in that youngling's path, believe me."

"Let's just hope the dragon doesn't set the forest on fire before you have your chance at him," Rhianne said.

Isa went to the bow, Nico on her heels, and they watched the Brunes' ship sail closer and closer to the island of the dryad elves. If the wards held, this whole thing would be over before it started.

CHAPTER 20

VIRIDI

Under the starry sky, the dryad elves gathered at the spring in the very heart of the island and chanted in the ancient tree tongue. Magic, flickering in shades of pine, grass, and pale lichen, shimmered from their mouths to the surface of the spring. Then the power floated in bands of pinprick light toward the island's spiritual boundary, an invisible line about a mile from the uneven shoreline.

But the bands of light dimmed as they rose into the air, the magic dissipating before it could create the wards that kept their island invisible and unapproachable to all but dryad elves.

The king's lips drew down and his cold gaze settled on Viridi's face. "Someone doesn't care to reset our wards…"

"We must," Viridi said, meeting his father's eyes. "If we don't," he said, addressing the gathered leaders of the tribes and the most powerful magic wielders on the island, "and others arrive, I may lose myself and end their lives. It is for the safety of innocents that we create these wards."

Father looked away from Viridi, seemingly satisfied that Viridi's magic wasn't the lacking element of this spell work. "If any of you have doubts or thoughts, please feel free to speak."

But no one did.

Felix's brow furrowed as he studied Viridi from across the circle of elves. Viridi cocked his head questioningly at his friend, and Felix raised both eyebrows, his lips pursed. Viridi shook his head a fraction to let Felix know that it wasn't Viridi. Felix bit his lip, then grimaced.

Viridi blinked. *Was* it his own magic holding back the ward casting?

He swallowed. Maybe his power was acting on his secret wish that Isa would return somehow and everything would be pleasant again. It was an ignorant wish and well he knew it. All day while he took rest in the jeweltree that looked over the ocean, he'd dreamed of her laugh, the fire of curiosity and life in her eyes, the strength in her spirit despite all she had been through at the hands of those other humans. The way she loved and protected Nico was incredibly admirable. He wished he could just have one more night of talking with her and holding her.

He shut his eyes. The failed magic was due to him and his heart.

"Let us try once more," he said, opening his eyes and refusing to look at Father. "This must be done."

But after five more attempts, it was clear that his magic refused to go against his heart.

"Guards," Father said as the last of the failed ward magic fizzled, "arrange a sentry at each of the shorelines. Make certain to report any ships passing. Everyone else, be vigilant. In this great time we cannot be vulnerable. Remember the prophecy. We can only hope it speaks of a time in the far future or to a past that we do not know."

A fire ends the dryad's reign. Watch for the fire, oh Thorned One.

The problem with the prophecy was that they had lost the full meaning of the old words. It was technically the same language, but the sounds and symbols had changed here and there, making the true meaning impossible to discern. And yes, he was the Thorned One. Not even he could deny that at this point. But there had been other Thorned Ones in the past. Would there be more like him in the future? There was no way to know or to figure out what exactly they meant by *fire*.

As the sun grew hot, the afternoon wearing on, Viridi shook himself awake inside the tree where he had been feeding. He blinked, feeling the soft pressure of the tree around him like a heavy cloak, the energy sifting into his flesh in a series of warm sparks. His body didn't want to leave yet, but he had to begin his dark chore before the others woke at dusk.

Steeling himself, he lurched forward, mentally breaking

from the tree's magical embrace. His body pushed through the tree's layers like a swimmer in the sea, until the daylight washed over him. Day was always too harsh, too bright. Like all dryad elves, he strongly preferred the night, the starlight, the moon. Even as the Thorned One, he hadn't escaped that proclivity.

Taking a deep breath and filling his lungs with salty, woodsy air, he walked toward the village, where everyone else in his tribe would be resting inside their home trees.

The warrior guard trees loomed in their circle around the three thrones, his father's and the others. He shut his eyes and pushed the emotions he had for her into a dark corner of his mind.

Opening them again, he set his mind to his task—to threaten his tribe and spread word that all dryad elves should flee this island and seek a home elsewhere. It wouldn't be easy. They could acclimate to new home trees in other locations. He knew that much from the old tales and the scrolls they had in the great library, but it would be incredibly taxing, and some might die before they managed it. But he knew what the trees wanted from him, from the Thorned One.

Complete dominance.

The jeweltrees didn't care about the dryad elves. They did as they had to, as the Source's magic commanded, for now, but once they took hold of his mind in full, they would revolt through his hands and his power. Why he had been created to do this, he didn't know. But the truth of it rang through his soul as consistently as the tides. Perhaps it was to help the dryad elves evolve. Other races had done so over the eons. The sea folk and the human descendants of the goddess Vahly had become humans, some of them water mages. The high elves of long ago had combined with the goddess's descendants and branched into mountain elves, fae, and his own kind. Maybe dryad elves were to become something greater. It wasn't a terrible thought. They were too sheltered and one-minded here in this isolated island kingdom. And Viridi knew he wasn't the only one who often longed to leave these shores and see new places, meet new people.

His gaze went to Felix's tree. The maple stood at the edge of the village beyond the cluster of vine-cloaked wooden night homes that they'd each crafted with their dryad magic, asking the trees for a roof, walls, bathing pools, and places to dine or cook with dryad fire.

Felix knew this was coming and he trusted Viridi that this was necessary.

Viridi prayed to the Source that he wasn't mistaken, then he shut his eyes and summoned the dark power simmering deep inside his soul.

Isa gripped the boat's side, digging her nails into the weather-softened wood, as Rhianne ordered the skiffs lowered. The anchor was in place and Werian called for all hands on deck.

So far, the magical barrier wasn't a problem. The island was visible—three round-topped mountains laced with dark forests and bordered in sparkling sand. Had Viridi and his people not mended the magic?

Down the shore line, the Brunes' ship docked near a spit of rocky land and the dragon flew circles overhead. The Brunes' men climbed down the rope ladders and readied to leap onto land. Isa tensed.

Would the barrier come alive now and set them on fire? Turn them to ash?

The sailors around her on Werian and Rhianne's ship paused to watch alongside Isa, Eamon's small eyes squinting against the sun and Werian cocking his horned head.

The Brunes' men jumped to the sandy rocks.

And stood, brushing themselves off.

"That's a disappointment," Werian said.

Isa sighed. They were going to have to fight now. No more easy outs. "I wish they'd been grilled like Khem kabobs."

Rhianne snorted a laugh and unsheathed her wand. "Let's see if I can make your wish come true."

"Are you in range?"

"Maybe." She thrust her wand into the air and whispered a few words. Bright magic shot from the wand's tip and bowed over the water.

Dame's whistle cut through the sound of the cresting waves and the shouts of the sailors. The dragon dove at the ship, then cut upward at the last moment. She, the dragon, had to be so frightened of Dame to obey in that manner. Dragons weren't easily cowed if everything she'd heard and read was true.

I wish I could help you, dragon, she thought.

It wasn't the creature's fault she was fighting on the Brunes' side.

Rhianne's magic fell short of the ship and Dame, the sparks dying in the white foam of the sea.

"I'll keep trying as you row to shore," Rhianne said to Werian.

He kissed her, dipping her backward dramatically. "Thank you, my warrior witch queen."

She smiled, then turned her focus to the first of the fight as Isa took her turn to slip over the ship's side and onto the ladder leading down to the bobbing skiff.

Twisting as she climbed down, she watched the Brunes' men charge into the forest, axes and swords in hand. She put her free hand to her stomach. Nico was nowhere to be seen in the chaos of disembarking. He was most likely at the prow, wanting a good view. She wanted to hug him one more time before leaving the ship, but maybe it was better that he was distracted. The skiff bobbed as she dropped onto one of the plank seats, a sailor giving her a hand. Sitting on the end near a slim sailor with no less than three large knives on his belt, she tried to steel herself for battle.

Isa ran over the beach, the afternoon sun making the sand blindingly bright. She glanced over her shoulder to see Werian loosing an arrow at the lapis-lazuli-blue dragon flying over the tree line near the Brunes' drop-off point. The dragon shrieked, shaking its sapphire wings, then it veered westward. Isa wasn't certain if it had been hit or merely scared off course temporarily. Werian nocked another arrow.

On the far side of their own skiff, Rhianne's magic crackled from the end of her wand and shot toward Dame Brune.

Where had Seigneur disappeared to?

John and Eamon could surely have run faster than her with their longer legs, but they kept pace with her as they wove through the thick forest and the tangling ferns. Dew soaked Isa's skirts and boots and her lungs burned with the effort of running and jumping.

"Do you feel anything?" Sweat dripped from John's stubbled chin as the big man drew up beside her.

Did she? "Not yet, I don't think. I truly hope I'm not dragging you two into something really, really bad."

"We like really bad," Eamon said, chuckling as they rounded a bubbling creek and rushed up a rise of rocky ground. "It's our usual."

John huffed a laugh and ducked under an oak's low limb. "Anything less is boring."

Isa shook her head and began to tell them about an adventure she'd had once before the indenture, but a shout and a wail stopped her. She went quiet.

Eamon pushed his hair out of his eyes. "What was that?"

"Something is happening at the village. I didn't see Seigneur Brune on the ship or the shore, so it might be him, attacking them with his crew."

The three of them started running again, heading toward the village.

"What could he use to fight these elves? The dragon is still over there..." John jerked his head.

Isa looked up to see the dragon making a wide circle over the beach where they'd pulled ashore. The creature roared and the sound carved a hole in Isa's middle. Legs trembling, she forced herself to keep on. She eyed the dragon again, and just before it disappeared behind the trees, she noticed a slash through its wing and a line of blood dripping through the air behind it.

"Seems like Prince Werian hit it again. What will it take to get that thing on the ground?" she asked.

"Dragons are the toughest of any creature," John said. "Our captain's job isn't an easy one."

They ran headlong into the dryad village, then stopped abruptly.

A massive oak had come to life and was ripping up homes and throwing people across the ground.

No, it wasn't a tree. It was Viridi.

His arms were lengthy branches with knife-sharp tips. Where his black hair had been, now there were only oaken leaves and tall, spindly twigs reaching from his head toward the forest canopy above. His legs and feet weren't elven anymore; they'd changed into trunks and roots that slid over the earth like great snakes, the sound horrifying and unlike anything she'd ever heard.

He spun toward them. His eyes had turned white again.

Going still, he stared at her. A shudder rippled through his tree form.

He opened his mouth, his lips dark wood. "Mine." His voice echoed through the forest and rumbled through Isa's ears. One of his branches shot out and grew around her like a cage, leaves sprouting everywhere. The scent of freshly turned earth was overpowering.

"No. Viridi. They're coming. The Brunes with their dragon and their fire. They're here. You have to fight them, not your own people. Viridi!"

A strange heat built in her chest and spread through her limbs. Her back ached like she'd been hit even though he'd only protected her in his mad way, not hurt her. She held out her hands to see her fingertips shift into emerald talons.

Gasping, she fell against the wooden cage. What was this feeling in her skin, her bones…?

Seigneur Brune and the rest of his force arrived, swords and daggers already cutting down elves. She pressed her face against the cage to watch Werian and many more fighting back. The sounds of screams and grunts turned her stomach as her vision blurred.

The heat inside her threatened to burn her to ash.

"Isa!" John's voice carried through the noise of fighting, of swords drawn and shouts and the thud of bodies hitting the ground.

Her body felt as if it was breaking apart at the seams. "Viridi!" she called out as she pounded on the trap formed by tree roots.

A crackle and hiss of fire sounded, then a hole appeared in the wooden cage. Rhianne was using her wand to burn Isa a way out. Once the sparking orange and purple flames worked a sizable opening, she squeezed through and was free. The magical fire didn't scorch her, thankfully.

Rhianne called out her name and pointed.

The dragon hovered above Isa, its scaled face shadowed by its flapping and injured wings.

Dragonfire rippled from its maw.

Viridi's sight was reduced to white and black, but the movement of any living thing was immediately apparent with the way his new eyes saw life. When something living spun or leapt or opened their mouth to shout, the gray and white shimmered a glittering black.

His ears reverberated with the voices of the trees.

End them all. Take it all. It is ours.

With an acrid taste on his tongue and the scent of rot in his nose, he ripped and tore and destroyed and beat down the dryad elves until they were fleeing. But others were here. Strangers. They smelled like the sea and like scents from another life.

He had seen someone who made him feel ... different.

Dragging his new body in a half circle, he saw a cage of wood, a trap he had made but had already forgotten.

What was in there?

"Viridi?" a melodious female voice called out.

His heart hit his chest hard, and for a moment his vision cleared and he saw color once again; he felt himself once again.

"Isa?" Was that her name?

Another shouted the female's name, another woman—a witch. She had burned his cage. Isa wriggled from the cage.

Destroy her. Remember the prophecy, the trees hissed.

A shadow darkened his view of Isa and he looked up to see fire raining down.

He didn't think. The cold of pure terror washed away the jeweltrees' voices and he lunged into the path of the flames.

The heat scorched him as he began to shift from his Thorned form back into a dryad elf. Pain lanced his sides and back. The dragon shrieked along with him and the heat abated as the view of Isa's wide eyes turned to darkness.

Isa screamed as Viridi fell onto her, and they crashed into the remnants of the wooden cage. Dragonfire rippled around them and the invisible chain of the fated mate bond tightened sharply in her chest. Was this her end and his too? Pain crawled over her body even though Viridi blocked the flames. She tried to breathe, spots dancing at the edges of her vision.

The dragon shrieked, then the fire ceased. Cool air wafted around her, Viridi, and the broken roots and branches. Viridi's skin faded to its original color and his lips were pink once more. He collapsed, hanging limply onto what was left of the cage.

The dragon dropped from the sky as Isa attempted to drag Viridi, now fully in his dryad elf form, away from the fighting. His tunic—somehow magically appearing after his shift—had been burned through along his back, and his trousers smoked. His skin was pink and blistered along his lower back, but he should have been far worse off. Perhaps his Thorned One's body made him far less susceptible to a burn?

Still, the pain had to be terrible if it had knocked him out.

"There!" Rhianne shouted above the mess of dryad elves, their crew, and the Brunes' crew fighting with fists, swords, and daggers. She pointed to a spot beyond the village. A roar echoed from the area. The dragon had fallen, but it was still alive, still able to produce dragonfire.

Werian leapt from an overturned table and shot multiple arrows in quick succession, cutting down three of the Brunes' men. Then the fae prince rushed toward the place where Rhianne had indicated.

What was he going to do about the dragon?

At least, Dame and her controlling whistle appeared to be gone. Hopefully, Rhianne had defeated her with the fire magic from her wand.

Isa settled Viridi under the shade of a low-branched pine, her heart aching. Once she had her dagger at the ready in case someone decided to come at her or Viridi, she turned to tuck his tangled hair behind his wood-tipped, pointed ear. Her eyes burned as she stroked his silken hair.

"Please," she murmured. "Don't die. We're just getting started."

His body moved up and down in an uneven breathing pattern that spoke to his pain.

"It's all your fault," a voice said.

Isa raised her head and was on her feet in a moment,

holding the blade between her and the dryad elf who stalked toward her. It was Helena—the woman Viridi had banished. Helena's slim fingers wrapped around the hilt of a short sword, and dark green leaves swirled over her left hand. What could basic dryad elven magic do exactly? Surely she wasn't as powerful as Viridi, but those leaves made this potential fight a lot more unpredictable.

The fighting moved out of the village and toward the path that led to the coast. Neither Werian or Rhianne were anywhere to be seen.

Isa was alone.

"What's my fault exactly?" she asked, lacing her words with venom. "The storm that threw me onto this island, or the fact that bad people exist? Just want to clarify so I know what to feel guilty over."

Helena's amethyst eyes flashed. "Sharp tongues need cutting."

"Try it." Isa gripped her knife more tightly, her fingers damp with perspiration.

Helena arced her sword toward Isa's head. Isa lunged forward and slashed at her abdomen at the same moment Helena flung magicked leaves into the air. The leaves flew at Isa's eyes and blocked her vision. She dropped back and fell over Viridi's legs. She'd cut Helena, but didn't know how deeply. Keeping hold of her dagger, she used her other hand to tear at the leaves spinning around her temples and eyes. Their edges scratched at her skin and tugged at her eyelids like they would blind her if she chanced a look.

Thinking quickly as she rolled over Viridi's legs to avoid

Helena's sword, Isa lifted Viridi's hand to her eyes and used his fingers to draw the swirling leaves away.

The leaves dropped into her lap and she opened her eyes to see Helena's mouth fall open. The dryad elf recovered quickly, and although she avoided injuring Viridi, she lunged for Isa, her blade catching the setting sun.

Isa threw herself to the side, narrowly dodging what would have been a mortal wound, then she leapt to her feet and ran toward where she guessed Werian and Rhianne were. She prayed no one would injure Viridi. The dryad elves wouldn't hurt him because he was their prince. Right? The Brunes and their crew would most likely think Viridi was dead already.

Rhianne shot dazzling sparks from her wand toward a dryad elf who went down in a heap. Then she aimed for a woman—Ursane.

Isa's stomach rolled. She tripped and her knife went flying.

Ursane stumbled to hide from Rhianne behind a beech, while the dryad elf moaned on the ground near the edge of the village.

Helena broke into a run toward Isa, her mouth wide as she shouted in her language. Isa rummaged through a pile of fallen leaves to find her knife, but the debris was too thick. Rhianne straightened her wand arm and hissed a spell.

Helena dropped dead not ten feet from Isa. The elven woman's eyes were wide open and Isa tried not to feel glad she was gone.

Gathering her wits and trembling, Isa rushed to Rhianne and Werian. Everything was happening so quickly. Her mind hadn't caught up.

"Viridi...he needs help." Her tongue felt too large for her mouth and she was shaking terribly.

Werian nodded gravely but put a finger to his lips and pointed to the dragon whose head was in his lap. "Gorgeous girl," he said to the dragon. "We've had a rough time of it lately, haven't we? It's understandable you would be jumpy and ready to destroy anyone who moves too quickly." He gave Isa a meaningful stare. Then he glanced up, looking first at Rhianne before visually searching the surrounding trees for possible attacks.

Isa reached out a tentative hand and stroked the dragon's midnight scales. They felt like old coins and were surprisingly warm. "Greetings, dragon."

The dragon blinked up at Isa and made a clicking, purring sort of sound.

"She likes you very much," Werian said, his eyes wide as he traded a look with Rhianne.

Rhianne crossed her arms. "Hmm. I wonder..."

Werian rubbed a spot behind one of the dragon's crystalline spikes. "All will be well. You rest and we'll take care of those terrible people." He gently eased her snout onto a bed of grasses, then he stood, Isa doing the same.

"Viridi is there." Isa pressed a hand to her stomach and tried to stop shaking.

"Is he...?" Werian's eyes were soft, and his voice careful.

"He's alive." She pointed. "Can you heal him?"

Werian asked Rhianne to stay with the dragon, and he walked quickly with Isa to where Viridi lay.

Viridi's beauty and courage stole her breath again. Not only had he risked his life to save her, he'd been fighting the monster inside of him the entire time. The bond between them vibrated and a tickling, warm feeling rose and fell inside her chest and stomach.

Glancing at her as if he might have noticed the catch in her breath, Werian went to one knee and set a hand against Viridi's shoulder, near some of the burns. Tiny pricks of light and a soft golden glow showed around Werian's hand.

Viridi stirred, his dark eyes flicking open, his thorned fingertips digging into the ivy that grew around the base of the pine.

CHAPTER 24
VIRIDI

"Isa?"

"I'm here."

Her voice shot heat through his blood and he was on his feet in a blink.

Prince Werian stepped away with a sad smile. "I'm going to check the village for the Brunes and their men." His hand went to his short sword and his gaze was alert though the sounds of fighting had died away.

Viridi swept Isa into his arms. He held her tightly, the leaves of his crown and the ones that grew along his collarbone and from his forearms encircling her gently. She smelled like a blessing, a spell, a promise—sweet and powerful.

He pressed his lips to hers.

Her mouth was so sweet and soft that he forgot everything but the joy she magically gave and the heat of want she roused in him. His whole body hummed with need as he drew his tongue over her upper lip. Cradling her face with his hands, careful not to injure her with his thorned fingers, he tilted her head back, and with his lips traced a slow line down the petal-soft length of her neck. She shivered—hopefully with pleasure.

Drawing back, he returned to reality, to the beauty and the grief of what had happened.

Tears glittered in her eyes. "Fated mates is such a wild adventure. And in the middle of all this ... this horror? It's madness."

"It's fate, Lady of the Sun. Love is a magic that none dare try to understand."

He took her hand and helped her through the rubble, over a ditch he'd most likely made when he had been in his other form, and then across Rom's broken vegetable cart.

Despite the joy of having Isa at his side, Viridi felt as though he hadn't fed in ages. His feet didn't want to move. There were no bodies here, but there would be in the forest where the fighting had gone quiet, where some had lost their struggle against the intruders. He hadn't killed anyone, he would have known if he had, somehow he knew that. But if they were dead, he wasn't innocent in the fact; he had been distracting them, trying to frighten them. Even if he had acted in hope of helping, he had been the cause of some of these deaths. Never would he forget this day.

Werian and Rhianne joined them, the dragon plodding along after Werian. They checked every home for survivors, talking quietly and gravely about what had happened and why Viridi had done what he had done. They found one youngling hiding in a closet inside Branch's home. It was Branch's son, Linden.

He bent low and extended a hand, hoping the child hadn't seen him in his Thorned One form. "Linden? It is safe to come out now. Let's go find your kin, all right?"

Isa, Werian, and Rhianne wouldn't know what he was saying, but they must have figured it out, because they joined in, gently giving the lad encouragement that he could most likely only comprehend by watching their kind smiles and seeing their outstretched hands.

Linden didn't smile, but he did crawl out. He immediately grasped Isa's leg and held on, closing his eyes and pressing his face into her skirts. She laughed sadly and ran a hand over Linden's head of fine blond hair, her fingers brushing his pointed ear. She didn't jerk away from his differences, but instead cooed at him like he was her own child. Viridi could see how the mother-son sort of relationship had formed between Isa and Nico. She had a way with young ones despite her occasionally sharp tongue and blunt manner.

When the five of them emerged from Branch's ruined home, they found a host of his people gathered in the debris of the village. Some had black blood still trickling from cuts along their arms or across their sides.

Showing a black eye and a bruised jaw, Felix hurried to Viridi and set a hand on his shoulder. "I'm here. No matter what."

"I don't deserve you, friend."

Branch waved at Linden and he ran to his father. Embracing Linden with a force that made Viridi's heart quake, Branch whispered to his son as tears ran down his cheeks. Viridi knew a bit of that emotion. It was how he'd felt when he'd awoken to Isa's face. He had feared she died and that he had been dreaming.

"Yes, you do. I know you have strong reasons for what happened today." Felix gave his shoulder a squeeze, then stepped back as Father approached.

"Ten of our own were murdered today." Fatigue drew Father's face into long lines and slashes. "Tell me, my son, what prompted you to side with those intruders and attack your own?" His features held the pinch of rage, but his eyes were sad, an emotion Viridi had never seen on his father until now.

"I didn't side with them. That was a terrible coincidence," Viridi said. The others talked with one another, narrowing their eyes at Viridi and Felix too. "I meant to show you exactly how it will be when I am fully the Thorned One and I no longer have control over my actions. You don't hear the trees. You don't realize that they are against us."

"But you are theirs. How could they be against you?"

Viridi shook his head sharply. "They want me to thrive, but they don't care for my heart and who I love. They are driven by some motivation I don't understand. I think perhaps we are meant to change or perhaps to be wiped from the Earth. Maybe our time is over, Father."

Father's eyes went cold. "No."

Viridi lifted his hands. "That was only the start of what is to come if I should survive. When they take my thoughts, all I see is their view. And they want to kill every last one of you."

"That cannot be." Father frowned and cocked his head. "Why are you lying?"

"I'm not. Why would I lie? What do I have to gain by terrorizing my own people?"

"You want the human woman. You want to reign in my place."

Viridi clenched his jaw. "I don't want what you want, Father. I'm not you. I don't thirst for power. I never have. You know this, but you refuse to believe that as well. I don't know what else to do. I tried to walk into the sea, but they pulled me back."

"Who?" Felix's voice was kind, but fear sharpened his tone.

"The trees. They took hold of my mind and body, forcing me to walk back to shore, keeping me from ending my life in order to save you all. If I leave this island, they will strike out at you. You must leave."

"I will never leave my island," Father said.

It was no surprise. "As for the second wave of intruders, I'll let Isa explain."

"They enslaved me and my ward, Nico. Seigneur Brune is a greedy, ruthless, cold man. He must believe there is treasure here. I don't think he would do so much to get Nico or me back. Besides, he wasn't focused on us during the fighting. It didn't seem that way to me anyhow. My guess is that he saw your island the same time I did, when the storm broke through your wards."

Father glared at Viridi and he knew he was thinking about Viridi's inability to help them rework those wards and how much of this was all his fault.

"I regret what happened here. I will mourn those we have lost. But I did as best I could have with what I know and with what I could control. This tragedy is not Isa's fault or my own. It is fate."

"The slaver is still on our land," Rom said loudly, his curly hair tossed by the wind and his eyes unblinking.

Viridi exhaled slowly, the weight of it all pressing down on his shoulders. "Let him have it. The trees will end what he has started."

Rom grinned wickedly and the rest joined in, Felix too.

But not Father.

He crossed his arms and set his gaze on Viridi, stare never wavering as Viridi and Isa detailed the suggestions that Werian and Rhianne had made if the others agreed to join in on the journey to another island.

They gathered what remained of their ruined belongings, small bags of pottery, books and scrolls, carved memory circles. The young ones took up whatever toys they could find in the rubble, their cheeks stained with dirt.

Viridi didn't even bother to return to his castle. All of his staff was here and he didn't want to look on a life he wouldn't be able to enjoy ever again. He had to look forward instead, forward to a life with Isa in a new place. If the trees would let him leave…

He prayed to the Source and the god Arcturus that leaving the cursed trees here wouldn't be the end of him. He prayed even more sincerely that it wouldn't be the end of anyone else.

At the shoreline, Werian and Rhianne helped everyone into the skiffs that John and Eamon had brought from the ship while Isa's mind twisted around what had happened when Viridi grew that cage around her.

Her fingers had turned to talons. Her skin had gone sparkling and odd...

She started to ask Viridi about it, but her mouth shut of its own accord. There was time enough to deal with that once they'd set sail. Surely, someone would know something helpful.

Thankfully, Werian seemed to have healed most of the injured crew, but he looked half dead himself.

"You've done too much, Prince Werian," Isa said.

"He has," Rhianne agreed.

Dark circles hung beneath Rhianne's eyes as well, and

she was favoring one leg as she crawled into the third skiff. They all needed time to heal.

Isa felt guilty for not being injured much at all. The only thing she'd suffered was a mild burn, and Werian had healed that completely.

"I'll be fine, my lovely ladies," Werian said. Isa could tell he was lying through his teeth. "Now, we must decide how to proceed."

Isa looked toward the ship, where Nico was safely hidden. The thought of him being curled up with the crew there made everything else survivable. "Has anyone seen Seigneur Brune?"

"No," Werian said, glancing back at the dragon before meeting her gaze. The dragon had apparently decided to remain with them. The poor creature was nearly as tired-looking as Werian. "What do you suggest we do?"

Isa frowned. "You're asking me? You're the royals who have fought in wars."

"I'm still asking you, yes," Werian said.

"Let's get everyone aboard and then talk about what to do. Do you agree, Prince Viridi?"

Viridi was staring at the forest, his back to the sea.

Her heart broke. Before she knew what she was doing, she was linking her hand in his and pressing her cheek to his arm. "We will just talk on board. Maybe there is another way to solve this."

Viridi nodded, and when Isa glanced at Rhianne and Werian, they gave her sympathetic looks.

Once all the dryad elves and sailors were on the skiffs,

they rowed away from the island and toward the ship. The dragon pushed away from the sand and soared into the sky, her wounds healed by Werian.

Isa kept an eye on the Brunes' ship. She saw a few figures moving about, but there was no way to know what they were up to.

At the ship, Eamon crawled out of their skiff first, then held the rope ladder steady as Isa scrambled up with Viridi close behind. On deck, sailors rushed here and there, rolling rope, talking over the compass box, and prepping the sails to hoist.

Viridi looked entirely miserable. "My lady," he said, giving her a sad smile, "go, embrace your youngling and hold him tightly."

She pressed a quick kiss to Viridi's cheek, then hurried belowdecks. Her feet pounded down the salt-worn steps, the wood groaning like she weighed far more than she did. Blinking, she squinted in the dark quarters where the pale shapes of hammocks swung. Barrels lined the sides of the ship. The door to the bilge pump hung open, the bronze fittings catching the light of two lanterns hung from posts.

"Nico!"

The hammocks were empty.

The sweet scent of pipe smoke had Isa turning and hurrying beyond the stairs. A sailor was tying a barrel to a ring in the ship's side.

"Who are you looking for, milady?" Another lantern swung slowly above his dark, curly hair.

"Nico. The young boy?" Her voice had gone thin and reedy.

"I haven't seen him since you all went ashore for the fighting."

A chill spread across Isa's flesh like she'd leapt into a winter sea, then a coal of searing heat glowed deep inside her. Her fingers tingled and she fisted them tightly.

No. Not right now. She could not deal with whatever her body was doing right now.

"Have you been aboard this whole time?" she asked the pipe-smoking sailor.

"Yes, milady." He took out the pipe and eyed her like she'd gone mad. "As the captain ordered me."

She tore back up the stairs, her foot slipping on the last one. Catching herself with one hand on the bronze railing, she shouted over the bustling crew and the injured sailors who were being hefted as carefully as was possible over the sides, "Nico!"

Viridi was at her side in a flash of movement surely only elves could manage. "He's not here?"

Rhianne looked at them and frowned. She leaned toward a crew member who was settling another three injured mates on deck. Rhianne then stood and raised a hand, getting the crew's attention. She held to a sail's line. "Anyone seen the boy?"

A man with a braided beard and massive shoulders stepped forward in respect to Rhianne. "He went ashore in a skiff like captain ordered."

Werian lowered his head, his gaze going dangerous. "I didn't make that order."

"He said..." the bearded man stumbled over his words. "...the boy said you wanted him in my skiff, to meet up with Mistress Isa."

"I'm not angry with you, Thomas," Werian said to the man while Isa's ears rang. "I'm worried about the situation."

Memories flooded Isa's mind: Nico holding her hand at the dock when they first boarded the Brunes' ship. His fingers were hardly more than bones. His bright blue eyes looking down at her and telling her a story he'd made up when she was sick for the first of a million times onboard. The ferocious protectiveness that gripped her when Ursane began beating him.

Then she imagined what might be happening now... "Seigneur has him. I just know it."

Isa fought off panic as Rhianne took out her wand, her fingers trembling with fatigue.

"No," Isa said. "You all must stay here and heal. We can handle this."

Viridi's eyes widened a fraction and he glanced toward the shore.

"Absolutely not," Werian said. "John and Eamon have things covered here. Princess Rhianne and I will be at your side, ready to fight as needed."

The dragon flew overhead and landed on deck gracefully, wings brushing the main mast and nearly taking out Eamon. Everyone froze.

"I had wondered what your choice would be," Werian said cautiously.

Sunlight sparkled over the ice-blue crystals that grew in a line down the dragon's spine. She tucked her wings, and her citrine gaze flicked to the sailor nearest her crystal-spiked tail. The man looked like he was about to be sick all over the deck.

"Careful now, crew," Werian said. "She has been treated poorly."

Isa remembered the butcher's dog who had lived just down the way from her family during her childhood. The butcher had tied the poor thing up on a short rope, and several of the town bullies would taunt the creature. She remembered one boy poking the dog roughly with a stick, hitting the dog's eye once. And she'd never forget the day the dog's rope broke. That boy with the stick had lost use of his left hand for good by the time the butcher pulled the dog off of him.

The dragon lowered its large head and eyed everyone in turn as if she were sizing them all up. Hopefully, as potential allies rather than possible meals.

Isa couldn't just stand there another minute. Nico was missing, and most likely in Seigneur Brune's terrible hands.

"Maybe she'd like a bit of food?" John started toward one of the many barrels.

The dragon jerked, eyes narrowing and belly going orange with banked fire.

"Easy now," Werian said, a hand out.

Isa walked ever so slowly toward the spot where the rope ladder was secured as the ship bobbed gently.

The wind rose and a wave crested. One of the dryad elves stumbled and fell onto the deck. The dragon snarled and swung around to face him and Werian launched himself between the dragon and the elf. With a hiss, the dragon snapped at Werian, catching his shoulder.

Blood poured from the wound and Werian paled further, Rhianne crying out.

"I'm fine," Werian said, a sheen of sweat on his forehead. "I'll be fine, little fox," he said to Rhianne. "She must realize we will not retaliate. That we are on her side."

"But your shoulder..." Isa started. Blood stained his entire tunic and the right side of his trousers now. If Werian had been human, he'd have already been dead.

The dragon glanced at Viridi, then looked him up and down like she wasn't sure about him.

He held out his hands and spoke in his language. The sounds were strange and lovely.

With an odd rumbling, the dragon closed her eyes and began making sounds at Viridi and then at Werian.

"Is she speaking to you?" Viridi asked Werian. "Can you understand her? I spoke to her in the dryad tongue."

"It's an old tongue and she understands it. I believe she is sorry for hurting me and for attempting to attack us all, if I am reading her sounds and body right. It's an old fae art and I am poorly out of practice."

The dragon huffed a breath that smelled like citrus and charcoal, then she curled up like a massive cat and promptly began snoring.

Viridi grinned and Werian chuckled as Rhianne shook her head.

"Stay here and heal, Prince Werian. Princess Rhianne, he needs you. I will go for Nico. Viridi will come with me."

"Are you sure?" Viridi asked.

"No, we must come with you," Rhianne said, but her attention was all on Werian.

Isa didn't hold it against her. Her husband was still bleeding profusely. "No. The two of us will find out what we can and make a plan."

Viridi's hand warmed her back as she climbed over the side of the ship. The rope ladder grated against her chapped palms as she hurried down to the bobbing skiff. Maybe Nico was simply off in the forest. Maybe she was jumping to terrible conclusions.

The two sailors in the skiff—one who looked like he'd been in the sun since the beginning of time, and the other who had ears like a hare's—listened as John ordered them to row Isa and Viridi ashore and to keep them accompanied as needed.

What was happening to Nico right now? Isa gripped the edges of the plank of rough-grained wood that served as one of the seats in the skiff.

Viridi's hand appeared on hers. She looked up into his dark, gorgeous eyes. "We will get him back."

"But..." There was definitely hesitation in his gaze.

He took a breath and looked away.

The sea grew angry and Isa and Viridi took up oars to help out the two sailors. Isa pulled on the oar as a wave lapped over the edge and soaked her boots and the bottom of her skirts. She still had ash under her fingernails from Viridi's clothing, and there were splinters in her thumb and palm from ... well, she wasn't sure, but the irritation blended into the aches and pains of the day's events. All of it was nothing to the way her stomach soured and twisted over her thoughts of Nico and what they could be doing to him.

If he was even alive.

She rowed harder, muscles crying out as she obeyed the quick commands of the sailors. The tide fought their struggle to reach the sand, but at last the skiff's bottom scraped the shore and they jumped out and looked toward the Brunes' ship.

The sun-tanned sailor set the last oar inside the skiff.

Isa studied the Brunes' ship, watching one man move up the mast and climb into the crow's nest. They were still anchored at that same line of rock that served as a dock. She could have sworn the man was looking at her, but it was much too far to know that.

Isa put a hand on one of the two long daggers Rhianne had given her. They were a comfort, but she hoped she wouldn't have to use them. She was rusty with fighting after serving the Brunes daily until her body refused to move. She couldn't simply walk up to the ship and ask if they had Nico. That was a good way to get killed.

Instead she veered toward the forest. They could take a less obvious route toward their pinnaces and ship, watching. Then they could decide how to manage this. Viridi could certainly do something with that wild power of his.

CHAPTER 27
VIRIDI

"I'm stunned there is such a crew of humans," Viridi said. "This is why my people must expand their horizons. We have never trusted humans, and hold far too many prejudices."

He kept talking about this and that, trying to stop the jeweltrees' whispering from growing too loud, too strong.

Take her. She would make you glow with energy if you took all of hers. You cannot fight your fate, Thorned One. Destined to rise and reign. Take her. Destroy them all.

Their whispers were in the ancient tongue; they spoke like branches snapping and leaves tearing in a storm. But even in their harshness, their voices pleased him deeply. He gritted his teeth in an effort to stop listening, to ignore their magic-infused demands.

Stop! he shouted silently from his mind to theirs. *I will never obey you. I will tear you from your roots if you continue this madness.*

The trees went silent in his head. Utterly silent. Then the wind rose, howling through the upper reaches of the sea cave near the turn on the shoreline, whipping across his face and tearing Isa's hair from its bindings.

They wouldn't turn on him, would they?

"I hate it when these ocean-swamped islands get wind like this," the weather-worn sailor shouted over the thrashing of the pines and the crack of the straining beeches and maples. "Takes the skin off my bones."

"Quiet, please," Viridi said. Isa glanced at him as she tugged a thick lock of dark hair from her face. "I hear voices. I think—"

A group of men crashed through the brush.

Isa's eyes seemed to flash and her skin shimmered oddly...

Seigneur Brune held Nico by the hair.

Heat sparked inside Isa's chest and spread through her entire body like a wildfire.

"Isa!" Nico called out, his voice full of pain.

She lunged, raging, but Viridi held her back. His gaze went from her to the knife Seigneur held in his other hand. Seigneur pulled Nico closer, the grip on his hair so tight that Seigneur's knuckles were white. A dark bruise ran along Nico's cheek, and he held his left arm like it might be injured.

Seigneur was going to die. That was it. No more hemming or hawing. Somehow, Isa would see that evil man's end and she would dance on his ashes. The heat inside her crackled and snapped and her vision went oddly clear and bright.

"I am prince of this island," Viridi said, his voice deep,

powerful. "What do you want in exchange for the human boy?"

"I want it all," Seigneur said, grinning, his trim beard twisting up at the corners of his lips. "Jewels. Scrolls. Everything in those two monstrous tree castles. I have men stationed at intervals around your island. If they don't get a message from me telling them to return to our ship by the time the moon is high, they will set their torches to your trees and finish off this island of legends," he said, his words grating.

Isa blinked, trying to see Nico, but the light was too bright or not bright enough...

More men broke through the trees carrying large wooden trunks that were bursting with pearl necklaces, golden chains, and age-darkened scrolls that probably contained some of the rarest knowledge in the world considering how old this civilization was.

"Now, get out of our way and head back to your ship," Seigneur said, sneering. "You're not going to attack me while I have this boy." He shook Nico hard and Nico yelped.

Isa's fingers prickled with heat and energy. "Release him and you can carry on with your pirating, you filthy beast."

Seigneur lifted his eyebrows and stuck out his bottom lip like a pouting child. "Oh, do you not understand, little mouse?"

Viridi stepped forward. Isa grabbed his hand. His thorned fingers had lengthened and the change was coming on.

Seigneur didn't bat an eye. "I will let *you* go, little mouse, because you're more trouble than you're worth, but this one is young enough that he can still be beaten into submission."

He smiled at Nico and the heat inside Isa exploded.

Light flashed around her body, blinding and star-bright; her limbs burned and stretched and cramped. She wasn't in pain, but her head spun. Her back ached, pressure building along her spine and shoulder blades. The pressure released and a rush of warmth spread over her skin. As the heat raged across her body, she shut her eyes and threw back her head, calling out for Viridi.

When she opened her eyes, Seigneur was running away with Nico in tow. Seigneur's men were firing arrows at her.

Moving by instinct, she leapt to block them.

The arrows bounced off her body, no pain at all. She thrashed, her mind completely tangled and her head dizzy. Something blocked the other two arrows, but then she turned quickly and Viridi shouted.

The sailors were wide-eyed and stumbling backward, one bleeding profusely from his temple and the other with a broken leg.

Viridi lay still on the ground, jaw loose, unconscious.

"What happened?" she tried to say, but her mouth wouldn't work and her thoughts were jumbled and incoherent.

Stepping toward Viridi, she halted, heart hammering wildly. Why was he so small or far away or...? She shook her head. She was so insanely confused.

Taking another step, she saw that her feet weren't in boots. And they weren't feet anymore. They were...

She had taloned toes. Emerald scales ran all the way up her legs. Stretching out her arms, she—

Wings unfurled from her body and she lifted her head, terror roaring from her lungs.

Mind whirling, she ran and leapt. Beating her wings, she rose into the air and flew higher and higher and higher, tears streaming down her scaled face.

Her thoughts scattered in the wind that dried her tears. Soon her mind was lost to watching the way the rising moon cast shadows over the island's range of soft mountains and black cliffs, along the twisting pines that lined the golden coast.

She felt as though she'd always been a dragon flying over an island.

The ocean glimmered in the silver light and she inhaled, taking in the scent of salty water, flowers in bloom, and the unique incense of the ancient forest below.

A face flashed through her mind. A crown of branches. Wood-tipped and pointed ears. Dark eyes and a slanting grin.

Viridi.

She spun from the sky, panicking. *How am I flying?* Why was she a dragon? Her heart was pounding right out of her ribs. She was so stars-blasted confused.

Catching a wing on a tree branch, she crashed into the forest and landed on her belly. There was a bright flash of light and she was human, naked and shaking.

Another face blinked through her mind. *Nico.*

"Nico!" she stood on trembling legs. Her arms shimmered with emerald scales along the backs of her hands and then again near her elbows.

Part human. Part dragon.

How had this happened to her? Had someone cursed her?

Viridi came running out of the deeper forest, the trees bowing to him as he passed. He whipped off his cloak and threw it around her shoulders before pulling her close and kissing her head.

"You are magnificent. Did you not know you are a dragon shifter?"

The warmth and love pouring from him through the fated mate bond was the best feeling she'd ever had. She put her lips to his and he kissed her back. His pointed tongue dusted over hers and her blood rushed hotly, warming her heart and her belly and lower. Her hands were in his tousled hair and she couldn't get close enough. The feel of his careful hands around her bare waist beneath the cloak was almost too much to withstand.

"Are you all right?" he breathed into her ear. "Did you not know?"

She pulled away, feeling whole again now that he was here beside her. "I didn't ... is that a thing people sometimes are? I heard that Prince Dorin of Balaur was a dragon shifter, but I thought he was the only one. They say his blood held dormant power that his close contact with the dragons and their magic had sparked to life and..." She swallowed, her throat raw.

"Here," he said stepping back. He whispered in his language and waved a hand over a tangle of ivy at the base of a split pine tree.

The vines slid up Isa's body, tickling, until they smoothed into what appeared to be some sort of cloth. The sides nipped in and soon she was wearing a long tunic with a vine belt and some leaf-green trousers.

"I saved these for you." Viridi held out the two daggers that Rhianne had given her.

Isa took them and tucked them into her new belt. "Everything since the storm has been part nightmare, part dream." She shook her head, unbelieving. "There is a part of me that knew this about myself though," she said, her thoughts going to her many dreams of dragons and her lifelong curiosity about her homelands.

Viridi smiled sadly.

"Regardless, there is no time to ponder it now." At least, she had more power with this wild development. "Nico needs us. Let's go destroy Seigneur Brune."

Her back sparked with heat and her wings appeared again, expanding past the borrowed cloak. It felt oddly familiar in a way similar to her bond with Viridi. She held one wing aloft to study it. The rest of her was still human, if not a little scaled here and there. The moonlight passed through the wing, turning the deep green to the hue of the sea under the summer sun. A thought occurred to her and she grinned.

"I like that grin," he said. "It looks like noble power."

She let the compliment sink in, relishing the feel of having power for once in her life. "I will fly over that arsehead's ship and see if I can light it on fire. You transform and use your power to defend and grab Nico while they are distracted."

"But what if I lose control?"

"You won't," she said.

"You don't know that. I don't know that."

"I don't know if I will either. I'm a dragon, for stones' sake. What in the name of all the gods am I supposed to do with this?" She laughed hysterically. "I just know that for some reason the Source has granted the both of us with these wild powers, and I aim to use them to kick some sense into the world. Listen, I believe in you. I feel your strength..." She touched the spot over her part human, part dragon heart. "Right here. Rouse the monster in you and put it to work, Prince."

He kissed her again, his lips somehow strong and soft at the same time. "My Lady of the Sun. Your fire inspires me. Let's go change Nico's fate."

Night wrapped the island tightly and the jeweltrees began to whisper again.

Feed, Thorned One. Rise and feed and draw the energy from all. This is the path of your fate. Do not turn your back on us.

The voices sounded sharper, and the words came more quickly, racing through his mind almost too jumbled to understand.

You must. Before it is too late. Must. Must. Destroy. End them. We will reign. No fire. Fire. Fire. Yes.

He frowned and rubbed a palm over his face. The trees weren't even making sense any longer. They were arguing among themselves and jumbling the old prophecy with their orders to him. He wished he could pry their voices out of his head, and it saddened him to feel that way. Trees were a dryad's life force, their twin life. Brushing his thorned fingers on an oak as he passed by, he grieved the hate his heart held for them.

Stars twinkled above the Brunes' ship, and the sound of arguing rose into the air. A woman's voice and a man's. With the waves lapping the shore, it was impossible to understand them.

Then Isa—half dragon and all his—soared between the ship and the crescent moon.

A smile stretched his lips. She was magnificent.

She'd not changed into her full dragon form, but instead flew with dragon wings on her human body.

Would she be able to summon dragonfire in this form?

She was such a wild, brave thing. After her first fear of what she was had passed, she had thrown herself into this new existence. She owned her true self.

Something stirred inside his chest. Envy? A gentle envy as he loved her so, the fated bond between them unshakable. And he was so very proud of her as she veered over the ship once more, a silent predator, confident and powerful.

A fine, fine mate.

Though he was cursed with his position as the Thorned One, the Source had also blessed him.

The dangerous shape of Isa filled with light and then fire erupted along the lashed-down mainsail. Chaos ensued. Voices rose in alarm and suddenly numerous humans were dashing this way and that in efforts to put out the fire.

Viridi kept to the cluster of oaks at the very edge of the beach, his boots dampened by the sea. He allowed himself to shift into his more powerful form, but then he stopped, pulling the magic deep inside again. His stomach twisted, the resistance nauseating.

His mind was filled with images of the village in ruins. Of the bruises and cuts he'd inflicted on his people. Of the horror in their eyes.

No. He would save Isa's Nico using his base dryad elf magic. That would have to be enough. He couldn't trust the Thorned One writhing just under his skin.

Breathing deeply, he drew energy from the earth under his boots and from the oak where his hand rested. Sparkling green magic flickered around his thorned fingertips, disappearing as the spell came to life.

The oaks' roots slithered across the rocky edge of the beach and grew quickly across the deep water at this side of the island. They stretched over the ocean cavern that he had once visited on a dark day, then the roots slid up the side of the Brunes' ship.

Viridi shut his eyes and let his dryad senses fall into the roots.

The scent of burning wood, fear-laced sweat, and rum filled his nose. The roots lifted up as he ordered them to search for the boy's scent.

And there it was. He smelled youth, new flesh and energy, as well as the scent of the boy's kingdom—ancient magic specific to that place far away, and a blend of herbs with which Viridi wasn't familiar.

Though the roots could scent, they could not help Viridi see. When he sensed the roots were secured around the boy's torso, he urged them to cradle him. Then Viridi tugged on the magic and the roots rushed back toward the beach with Nico safely in tow, caged gently in lengths of oaken tendrils and shrouded by the night.

A sharp pain flashed up through the earth and into Viridi's body. He thrashed and lost contact with the trees' power.

Nico lay on the beach at the feet of three men. The moon and stars blinked across their axes.

They'd cut the roots and severed the magical bond. They had Nico in hand.

CHAPTER 30
ISA

Heart shattering—Viridi had been so close to getting Nico to safety—Isa flew overhead and blew fire into the air. She couldn't strike. Nico was too close. She would burn him too.

A woman came running out of the bowels of the ship shouting.

It was Dame. She wasn't dead.

Yet.

Dame, and Ursane the horrible thing, were struggling with something in their arms—a crossbow and a quiver of bolts. Chills raked Isa as she dodged two arrows from Seigneur's crew. Tendrils of amethyst and black magic soared from the direction of Werian's ship—Rhianne's spells. They were doing their best to help out.

Another volley of arrows. Isa tilted her wings and used her arms to move in a rising air current, but she was new to this and definitely no expert.

Well, she had to try something.

She swooped down toward Nico, desperate to snag him and somehow fly him out of the reach of the Brunes and their men.

Pain jolted through her. A tear in her wing.

She plummeted to the ground and hit hard, the breath leaving her lungs in a rush.

A crossbow bolt jutted from the moonlit sand a foot from her and she forced herself to her knees. Sweat poured from her face as the agony ricocheted through her body. Wings might be amazing in some ways, but they were obviously incredibly sensitive.

A groan burst from her lips as she managed to stand on shaking legs, sand in her mouth and eyes.

"Let him go!" she roared at the men. She lifted her head and breathed fire into the sky, her anger and frustration as painful as the injury to her wing.

Dame, Ursane, and Seigneur walked over the rocks and sand toward the men who held Nico.

Dame smiled, the moonlight reflecting off her teeth as she handed the crossbow to Seigneur. Ursane crossed her arms and glared. Dame grabbed Nico by the neck and forced him to kneel. He looked at Isa. Tears silvered the edges of his eyes. His fingers dug into Dame's arm and Isa wished to press a soft, healing kiss onto every dry one of his knobby knuckles.

She was going to lose him.

A bottomless darkness opened inside her and she gasped, unable to take a breath. They were going to cut his throat and she was going to be stuck here with talons and fire and wings that could do nothing.

A sob choked her.

Wait. She had options. She had power here. "If you kill him," she said, pushing back at the panic and the pain in her wing, "I will immediately end you all. I don't care if you take me down along the way. You are finished if you don't give him to me, healthy and whole."

Seigneur loaded the crossbow. "Let's see you try." He nodded at Dame.

A crack sounded behind Isa.

Viridi thought through the agony that the sudden severing of his bond with the trees had burned into him. His vision fogged and he leaned against one of the oaks, pulling breath into his shuddering lungs.

Isa couldn't do this alone.

He had to transform. *Fully*. Only with his full power could they hope to somehow free Nico without them killing him first.

Father appeared from the forest. "Destroy them all, my son. Everything will return to peace and happiness if you let go of that human woman and that boy and be who the jeweltrees insist you are."

"I know who I am. And peace and happiness are not the result of hiding from the world and shutting loved ones from your heart. Isa is my mate."

"Such a terrible disappointment." Father threw something silver.

Viridi raised his arm; tough bark grew over his flesh and deflected the short sword. The weapon bounced wildly back and lodged in Father's thigh. Blood spurted from the wound and Father dropped to the sand, blood spreading like roots beneath him.

"You created your own fate," Viridi said through gritted teeth. Unshed tears seared his eyes and he felt as though he were falling apart.

Blood blackened the sparkling sand at Father's feet. He jerked. His eyes widened and he fell onto his back, his chest heaving.

Viridi swallowed bile and reached out a hand. "Father, I..."

But Father's chest stilled.

The king was dead.

Cold washed over Viridi. The voices of the jeweltrees hissed louder and louder as the sensation of change shivered over Viridi's flesh and snapped and crackled along his bones. The magic surged through him and he felt like he was every tree in the world, every leaf and branch and root. He let the power wash through him completely, but he silently repeated Isa's words, holding them clear and bright as the ringing of a wind chime.

I feel your strength... Isa's voice said in his memory. *Rouse the monster in you and put it to work, Prince.*

That was the key she'd given him. Stop trying to hold back the horror and instead claim it as his own.

Destroy... The trees began rumbling in his ears, their

voices blending into one powerful force that was difficult to keep separate from his own mind.

"I am the Thorned One," Viridi repeated, now saying it out loud. "I know my own mind and my heart. Bend and bow." He focused on the forest behind him as branches extended from his fingers and head in snapping bursts, as his limbs grew stronger and stronger. "Bend and bow to me."

The jeweltrees warred with him, magic tugging at his arms and legs, at the roots that were now his feet and toes. Bright green magic, spun with a sickly yellow-white hue, whirled around him like a storm, tearing at his hair and nipping at him like thousands of small teeth. The scent of abhorrent magic hit his nose, sour and pungent.

He had seen magic that color once before—when the pirate witch had thrown her spells. His guess had been right. This was a curse she'd set on the jeweltrees.

Without his will, his branched arm shot out toward Isa.

He saw red, the blood he would take.

He saw fire, the energy he would drain, he would absorb.

Shaking his head, he lifted his chin to the stars. "I am the Thorned One."

The sickly yellowish color faded.

"I rule here. Not the trees. Not the witch's curse. I rule this island." Imagining his hands reaching around his own head and heart, he claimed the power, his fate, and the magic that wove him into who he was. "I. Am. The. Thorned. One."

The scent of rot dissipated. The pale yellow haze fizzled

away completely. The earth beneath him quaked and he went cold all over, frozen to stillness.

Then a burst of warmth shot from his chest, from his heart, to spread over his body. His vision cleared, the stars sparkling, blurring as he moved his gaze to Isa.

The jeweltrees sighed inside his mind and any signs of the pirate witch's curse disappeared.

Claiming his power had broken the dark magic.

He whipped his branches and roots around, then snared the Brunes and those who served them, lifting them all into the air. The crossbow dropped to the sand, a sword falling beside it.

Isa ran to Nico and held him tightly. She looked up at Viridi. "There is my monster mate. I knew you could do it."

Viridi gripped Isa's enemies tightly. "Do you wish for me to end them?"

Her wings shuffled, the injured one slower and making her wince. "No. Put them on their new ship and send them on their way. But first, I will mark them as slavers so no one will fall for their tricks again."

He lowered them to the sand, holding them firmly. Keeping Nico beside her, she removed one of her daggers. Fire glowed in her throat and she blew a small stream onto the end of the blade. Then on each of their foreheads, she drew an S in the common tongue's alphabet, indicating they were slavers. It was a mark Viridi had seen on one of the pirates who'd attacked during his childhood, a symbol known through the kingdoms, no doubt.

"Will you see that they go to their ship immediately?" she asked Viridi, fire still sparking from her lips.

He glared at the three people who had dared to treat his mate and her youngling poorly. "As you wish, Lady of the Sun."

"Thank you, Lord of the Stars." Her smile was life.

EPILOGUE

Isa

One Moon Later

Wings tucked, Queen Isa sat on her own wooden throne, her oak leaf gown draping across the feasting area's exposed roots and rich mosses. Dryad fires glowed, their spring-green light reflecting off Nico's smile as he ran from table to table, trying every new recipe that Felix and Werian had cooked up. Nico waved at her.

Isa adjusted her crown of branches and winked before nodding to yet another of the southern tribesmen, another guest here to promise fealty to her and to her king, Viridi.

The wedding had been a simple affair, hands bound with ivy and oak leaves, words spoken in the dryad elf tongue and in an older language still. She'd been so excited that the whole event was a blur. She'd need time to remember every second and to appreciate it all.

Now, John and Eamon were having a drinking contest, and if their unsteady stances were any clue, Dew was defeating them handily.

The visiting tribesmen and women walked away, smiling and murmuring—no doubt gossiping a bit about Isa, her scaled cheeks, taloned fingers, and of course ... the wings. She didn't mind it. At least she wasn't dull, and no one could say her life hadn't turned out truly adventurous. Besides, if anyone else tried to harm Nico, she had dragonfire, as well as an incredibly powerful dryad elf king, to back her up.

Viridi walked up, his mossy black cloak dragging the ground. "Enjoying yourself, my lovely mate?" He swept low for a kiss, his thorned fingers carefully cupping her chin.

Heat spread across her chest and stomach. He broke away before she'd had her fill.

"I am," she answered. "When do your wedding rituals end?"

Music floated through the air as the dryad elves, Werian, Rhianne, and the crew danced and laughed.

Lifting Isa's hand, Viridi eyed her with a dark, sultry gaze. "Are you asking when this feast will end and we will consummate our bond?" His branched crown stood almost a foot over his tangled black hair. He was truly a king from the legends, frightening and beautiful.

And all hers.

"I am." She blushed, and didn't care if everyone saw it.

Felix and Rom, two of Viridi's closest friends, were growing some sort of hammock made entirely of leaves for Nico, who leapt inside before it was complete and had to be caught by Dew. Isa heard this was Dew's first appearance at a feasting party. She didn't think it would be the hermit's last.

"I think it's past time we take our leave, Lady of the Sun," Viridi said quietly to Isa.

And so they did.

WITHIN THE OAKEN WALLS OF HIS CASTLE, VIRIDI LED ISA to his bedchamber. Her stomach lifted pleasantly in anticipation and her body tingled from head to toe. They walked through the ivy hanging over the room's archway and he waved his thorned fingers. The ivy thickened and the oak of the framing came together to form a woven door of sorts.

The idea that he wanted privacy sent flames through her blood.

His bed was round, woven of living oaks and pines that stood around the cushions and leafy blankets like sentries. Dusky green needles and smooth oak leaves filtered the soft, emerald light from the five dryad sconces set into the walls.

He removed his crown and hers, placing them on the side table. He sat on the bed and pulled her on top of him, his sharp fingers grazing her skin gently.

He was gloriously monstrous.

She untied his tunic until his powerful chest and flat stomach were open to her kisses. Running her mouth over his smooth skin, she inhaled his scent—crushed leaves and nectar. He groaned and drew her upward for a kiss. He nipped her throat with his sharp teeth and made that unusual sound she'd first heard when he'd transformed. Now, Viridi was a blend of both dryad elf and Thorned One, just as she was a mix of human and dragon. They were different; neither of them fit neatly into a category. And it was perfect.

His tongue lapped over her earlobe and his talons grazed one of her wings, sending blasts of tingling heat through her blood. She couldn't catch her breath. Her heart beat in every corner of her body, and stars save her, she wanted him so badly she could hardly keep from begging for him to be closer, closer still.

He hummed into the base of her throat as if he could guess what she was feeling and it pleased him. Wrapping his arms tightly around her, he lifted her suddenly. She eased her wings open and gasped as he set her against one of the trees, his hands rucking up her dress, his palms hot on her thighs. He kissed her collarbone and lower, every movement a joy and a pleasure like nothing she'd ever felt. With his body crushed to hers, she curled her fingers into his hair as he blessed her skin with kiss after kiss. His hips shifted as he took her weight into his arms and she shuddered. He lay her on the bed, her wings spread wide behind her, and he took one of her legs and began to dust her knee with presses of his soft lips.

. . .

Viridi couldn't get enough of the taste of her sweet skin or her sounds of delight. He lowered himself over her as she tucked her wings slightly. Leaning on his elbow, he drew his hand so very slowly over her curves, savoring her shuddering breath. He felt as though he'd swallowed starlight, his body alight with energy from tip to toe. Then he set his full weight on her and grabbed her leg to hook it over his hip. He spoke into her petal-soft throat.

"You are mine, Dragon Queen Isa. I will spend my days and nights discovering new ways to savor this fated bond between us."

"You are mine, Dryad King Viridi. I will spend my days and nights allowing you to do just that." She grinned wickedly and his heart soared.

The prophecy had spoken of her, his mate, the one with fire. Although inadvertently, she had helped him end the dryad's reign—his evil father's reign. All along, the prophecy had actually been a message of hope.

"My sun," he whispered.

He kissed her softly, tenderly, as his body hummed with need.

"My starlight," she answered.

His cursed life had become a blessing. He would never stop thanking the Source for the adventure of loving his Lady of the Sun.

. . .

Readers,

I hope you enjoyed Viridi and Isa's story! To read their bonus wedding scene, join my newsletter at https://www.alishaklapheke.com/free-prequel-1

Also, check out the other fantasy romance standalone novels in the Kingdoms of Lore series:

Enchanting the Elven Mage

Enchanting the Fae Prince

Enchanting the Dragon Lord

Thanks for reading!

Alisha